God of the Sullied

Other books by Gaurav Sharma

The Indian Story of an Author
Gone are the Days

God of the Sullied

Gaurav Sharma

Think Tank™
BOOKS

First published in 2018 by Think Tank Books™, New Delhi
Website: thinktankbooks.com
Email: editorial@thinktankbooks.com

Gaurav Sharma asserts the moral right to be identified as this book's author.

Illustrations by:
Pallavi Aman Singh - Farewell forever, Animals escaping & The lost legion.
Prabal Moudgil - Brahmin taming goat, Acharya-Eklavya debate, Eklavya knocking doors, Crowning liturgy of Eklavya & Children collecting coins.

This is a work of fiction. Names, characters, places and incidents are either the product of the author's imagination or are used fictitiously, and any resemblance to any actual persons, living or dead, events or locales, is entirely coincidental.

ISBN: 978-81-936204-4-1   eISBN: 978-81-936204-5-8
Price: INR 225/-   Price: INR 100/-
Maximum retail price of this book listed is only for the Indian subcontinent.
Selling price may vary elsewhere.

First Impression 2018   10 9 8 7 6 5 4 3 2 1

Praise for 'God of the Sullied'

'Gaurav puts a deliciously different taste in his stories.'
- Outlook

'Fast-paced, intriguing and engaging, this story is a complete page-turner.'
- The New Indian Express

'It is not often that writers manage to make the mythic interesting in modern times. Sharma's 'God of the Sullied', excels in bringing a paced narrative that compels readers to leaf through the pages till the very end. It's a sure shot page-turner.'
- Deccan Chronicle

'A classic, timeless work that sheds light on the ancient Indian philosophy and history. It's a gripping tale that is laced with freshly brewed twists and turns that keep the reader hooked till the last page.'
- United News of India

'A fascinating foray into loss, grief, deception and self-identity in a real and raw fashion. A fiction thriller so gripping in its action and so convincing in its accuracy that arithmetic appears gloomy.'
- Femonomic.com

Dada Ji, I seek your blessings.
&
Richa, I dedicate this book to you.

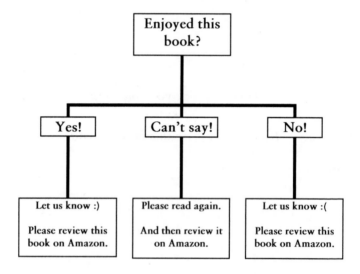

About the Author

Gaurav Sharma is a Delhi-born, Bihar-raised and Canada-based writer. He studied business at Langara College, Vancouver and journalism at Guru Gobind Singh Indraprastha University, New Delhi.

After writing three textbooks related to mass communication, Gaurav authored *Gone are the Days* (semi-autobiographical fiction) in 2016 and **The Indian Story of an Author** (creative nonfiction) in 2018. *God of the Sullied* is his second fiction. His upcoming novel would be *Long Live the Sullied*, a sequel to this book.

Gaurav likes playing chess and video games on PlayStation. To know more, connect with him on social media, reach out via his website authorgauravsharma.com, find him on Wikipedia or just Google his name. Something will come up, we promise!

Acknowledgements

Time for some formalities... who's going to read it anyway? ~~First and foremost, I would like to thank God~~. Err, I am an atheist.

Ishani, I can't thank you enough for showing faith in my work and help me take it closer to perfection.

Thank you, dear readers, for buying God of the Sullied. I hope you'll read its sequel, Long Live the Sullied too. Stay tuned to know when it's coming.

Thanks, Inderjeet, for beta reading the manuscript. You are the first and will remain the only one in Canada to do that. Yay!

Kudos to Kauldher family for letting me feel at home while being away from my home. I would like to mention *Nani Ma* and *Nana Ji* for always wanting the best for me. Many thanks to Amrita, Anisha and Anjali for maintaining a constructive environment at home.

Thank you, Pallavi for making illustrations for this book. You sketch like a pro. Also, many thanks for the editorial feedback.

High five to Aman, my brother. You were no help in writing this book, and that's why it was completed ahead of the time.

Dear Prabal, I can't forget your quirky ideas for promoting my book(s). Many thanks for doing the illustrations and making this book elegant in appearance.

Honorary mention for Chunnu and Chhotu, for everything but book-related. Oh! I forgot to write Disha and Soham and wrote your nicknames instead.

Thank you, Rashmi for taking care of the tax works for this otherwise poor author.

And Leema, even the Microsoft Word puts a red line under your name. So, you are not at all acknowledged here. We'll have a chat about it on the phone.

Thank you, Luvy for always being supportive throughout the writing process. More power to you on being best of the friend.

I now acknowledge the presence of evil inside me for it sometimes takes hostage of my mind, making me realise the virtue of being righteous.

Finally, I am indebted to *Vidya* for becoming an influence in my life. *Vidya,* an epithet of Goddess Saraswati, without whom this book would be in my mind only.

Welcome to God of the Sullied. Happy Reading!

Glossary

Aatma	: Soul
Acharya	: Teacher / Preceptor
Advaita-Vedanta	: A religious principle to spiritual realisation
Amma	: An older woman (proper noun in the book)
Antim-Dham	: Ultimate abode
Asatya	: Untruth / Falsehood
Asura	: Superhuman demigods
Avidya	: Ignorance / Illusion / Lack of knowledge
Brahmacharya	: Going after the highest universal principle
Brahman	: The highest universal principle
Brahma-Gyani	: One with the knowledge of Brahman
Brahmin	: One of the social classes in Hinduism
Choupal	: Community space in (Indian) villages
Devata	: Hindu deity
Gurukul	: Educational institution
Ji	: A suffix used with names to denote respect
Jiva	: All living beings
Jyotish-Acharyas	: Astrologers
Kali	: The evil
Kali-Yuga	: Era of the evil (last age per Hindu scriptures)
Kshatriya	: One of the social classes in Hinduism
Lagna	: Ascendant (astrological term)

Mata	: Sanskrit / Hindi word for mother
Maha-Mantri	: Chief minister of the kingdom
Maha-Purohit	: High priest
Maharaj	: Colloquial word for the king
Mathas	: Religious monasteries in Hinduism
Mujra	: Dance performed by females
Nakshatra	: Lunar mansion
Param-Aatma	: Supreme soul (denotes God)
Patala	: Netherworld
Purushottam	: Best humanist
Rishi	: Sage
Sadhna	: Practices leading to spiritual perfection
Samadhi	: State of meditative consciousness
Sannyasa	: Ascetics
Sarpanch	: Head of the village council
Shamshan	: Cremation ground
Shudra	: One of the social classes in Hinduism
Swarga	: One of the eight higher abodes
Trishula	: Trident (weapon)
Vaidya	: Medic / Physician
Varna	: Social class
Vidya	: Knowledge / Wisdom

Prologue

I was born along with the *Brahman*. I was there when nothing was, I am here when nothing is, and I will be present in all years to come.

Since time immemorial, there have been conquests to rule the planet earth. Many epochs ago, *devatas* and *asuras* ruled the land, but they couldn't adapt to the changing times. And so, many of them perished and remaining sought refuge in the *swarga* and *patala*. Then humans, the direct sons and daughters of the almighty God dominated the world. And hence began one such conquest which saw many civilisations rise and fall.

Magadha Kingdom's pride and then the Mauryan's might, the Kurus rose their empire to the power and then Mughals saw the sun set on them. And I have been a witness to all of this for I am immortal and neutral. All these civilisations, empires and dynasties learnt how to conquer but could never learn how to sustain their victories by changing with time. And those who don't learn how to change with the times, get replaced by the time.

Before I tell you, how bright the future will be, I want to ask if you are ready to evolve with the time? If yes, then behind yesterday's success, today's victory and tomorrow's conquests there is only one strategy, and that is, change. Change, first in your thoughts and then in your actions. If you are with me, then the time is on your side. Then whatever the times may be, you will succeed.

And once again, today the time is changing. I stand still, to tell you the story of the rise of the 'Sullied' in *Kali Yuga*, a tiny fraction of my eternal span. Get along with me as I don't wait for anybody. I am time, and I welcome you to the world of *Kali* where nothing is as it seems.

1: The Age of Kali

TIME

People suffered in great pain as peace dropped down tremendously. Incidents of friction and wrath tormented the world, turning the laws of nature and karma upside down with the evolution of the age of 'Kali'.

The sudden demise of Adi Shankaracharya in the early ninth century fostered turbulence in *mathas* established by him across the nation, which in turn propelled the rise of *Kali Yuga* in the holy lands of the Indian subcontinent.

Believers of corruption and violence arose, killing the truthful and good-natured. Dharma and its concept of central importance became superficial day by day as humanity proved itself to be the absolute blunder of humankind. The principles of religion were observed only for the sake of reputation as people put aside their holy books and their teachings. Sick people clutched in the hands of *Kali* gracefully did wrong to others, and man lived as if he would never die, died as he had never really lived. The world engaged in a race to make money and more money, as it became the new God of the era of sinners. Nature maligned herself with the dirt of inhumane practices and filth created by so-called human beings. Those who knew nothing about religion mounted on high seats, presuming to speak on religious principles. Since there was a tremendous and vicious outbreak of evil across the planet, this world howled in need of a Messiah.

It dated to the middle of the ninth century when mortals engulfed in the hodgepodge of ruining their present for making future secured, a handful of Ikshvakus somewhere in Rudraputra region of India planned their present better to strengthen future. Being afraid of the degraded society and filth of its people, most of them didn't reveal their identity to others whereas, remaining never knew that they descended from the great dynasty of Ikshvaku. It is said that Ikshvaku, the clan of Lord Ram and Buddha was one of the most prominent regimes in India. In those peak times of *Kali Yuga*, it seemed almost impossible for human beings to become like Lord Ram or Buddha. But the legacy of Ikshvakus stood still, as powerful as it was in the days of the Lords. They were less in quantity but integral in quality.

Amidst all this ruckus, lived a noble and wise man, Vyas in a small village of Rudraputra. Vyas - a descendant of Ikshvaku clan and a *Brahmin* by knowledge, *Kshatriya* by strength, *Vaishya* by hard work and *Shudra* by his service to humanity, was venerated as a saint without being a saint by profession. He never helped others with auspicious rituals and rites as such. Indeed, his thoughts and deeds made him a saint. Doing charities was his karma for he was devoted to standing for the public good. Vyas was no less than a *Purushottam*. A *Purushottam* of the dark epoch, an era where sinners judge and punish sinners for sinning differently.

2: The Prophecy

~~~

TIME

"What do you suggest; what does it seem like, *Maha-Purohit Ji?*" calmly asked Vyas with an anxious mind. Gently stroking his tangled white beard, *Maha-Purohit* uttered nothing and with a thoughtful gaze, looked momentarily into Vyas's eyes and was again lost in some intense astrological equations and combinations. Vyas became quite concerned, finding *Maha-Purohit* struggling with those formulas. Although he learned to implement total control over his mind and thoughts with regular meditation and *sadhana* yet the matter, this time, was of great importance and held tremendous significance in his life. Distracted by the ocean of questions raging inside his mind, Vyas couldn't fetch any thoughtful reflections at that moment.

Maha-Purohit would soon predict the time, day and nature of the birth of Vyas and Sumati's first child. He was the only guru of all prominent astrologers and *Jyotish-Acharyas* in Rudraputra and arrived to bless the family upon the request of some elders and close relatives as soon as they knew that the couple was expecting a baby.

Those were the days when in Rudraputra, childbirth was considered as a boon and blessing from the Almighty to the entire clan of the child. New-borns were given utmost importance and priority as they were the ones who would carry forward the legacy of the Ikshvaku dynasty.

Maha-Purohit desired for solitude and was left alone in a house with his astrological documents. The house, made up of wood and clay outlasted the others. Streaks of sunrays passing through one of the two broken windows lit up space inside the room. On the outside, gathered a crowd of people eagerly waiting for him to come out. Some were excited and optimistic while others thoughtful and concerned about the prediction to be made. Nobody saw *Maha-Purohit* so engulfed and captured with the astrological prophecies before. They were worried, expressing different opinions to the delay of prophecy for baby's birth. Vyas and Sumati no matter how intense the situation became were at their peace of mind. Whatever may happen, shall happen with the will of the Almighty.

The sun set in Rudraputra, leaving behind a thin stripe of scarlet in the horizon. It was soon heard that *Maha-Purohit* was ready with the predictions. Everybody gathered around a *choupal* where *Maha-Purohit* sat with some other Jyotish-*Acharya*s. They all ate evening breakfast prepared by the community to express their respect and gratitude towards those learned men. Vyas and Sumati climbed upon the dais and sat together, holding each other's hand, their fingers intertwined. After finish eating his breakfast, *Maha-Purohit* stood up taking a deep breath. Villagers became quiet and paid attention to what he would say.

"My heartiest greetings to all the inhabitants of Rudraputra! Thank you for the delicious food. I spent my whole life serving you in this privileged position of the *Maha-Purohit*. In my entire work history, I never came across such ad hoc arrangement of planets and *nakshatras* as I observed today while determining the time, day and nature of the birth of Vyas's child. Swati and Krittika *nakshatra* will form a unique alignment together with each other. The north star will shift its position towards Ursa Major constellation. Venus and the Moon will come closer in a retrograde motion concerning earth which will create strong winds and high tides. It happens once in a thousand years!

On the night of the next full moon, Sumati will give birth to a divine child. It will be a baby boy. The entire region will witness a wave of contentment after the birth of that child. Vyas will be blessed with prosperity. The child would be known for his compassion and will to serve humanity. However, there will come, a time when the child's views and actions will go opposite to what is deemed 'fit' in this society. There will be a time when he will try to destroy social stigma and traditional practices for the greater good of the world. It would be then when he is out-casted from this society and by its people, it is my understanding. With Sun, Jupiter and Moon sitting in his first, second and third house of *lagna*, this boy will demonstrate exemplary character. The scion of Ikshvaku will be born to fulfil God's will of protecting the righteous.

He will rise to power and influence. His birth may not be unique, but his death will create history.

What's more? The child will possess incredible willpower and knowledge to learn every type of skill and competence. He would have the ability to learn archery and other combat skills just by watching. Hence the name of the child shall be Eklavya! Eklavya, he who learns bow by watching. Prepare for his arrival, we all shall celebrate and welcome him with great pomp and show! My best wishes for Vyas and Sumati," *Maha-Purohit* said so and left. Moments later, he mystically disappeared into the darkness.

The villagers filled with joy after listening to the predictions as the birth of the son of Ikshvaku made everybody's day. They greeted each other and conveyed their best wishes to the couple. Despite a little worried about Eklavya's future, Vyas and Sumati were optimistic, hoping that their child would not be out-casted from the society. Nobody could accurately foresee what was about to happen.

One beautiful morning, seeing Vyas worried about something, Sumati asked the cause of his anxiety. Vyas told his wife of the trip to a neighbouring village to get some special seeds for the crops. Vyas in his heart of hearts didn't want to leave his pregnant wife alone in that vulnerable state. The neighbouring village, located about 30 kilometres away from their home, made the road journey of about five long hours. Lack of better means left Vyas with the only option to travel by bullock cart. There lay the mighty river Ganga in between those villages. There were few sailors from both the sides with small boats and canoes which carried commuters, helping them with their journey across the vast channel of the river. Sometimes, people waited for long hours to get in the vessel. Vyas needed those seeds to grow new wheat crops in his fields. Without the seeds, there could be no agriculture, something that was undesirable to him. Despite knowing that it could take God knows how much time for Vyas to return to home, Sumati advised him to head to the village, understanding the situation and endorsing the course of action her husband thought to take. Vyas contemplated for a while and with his unsettled mind led to the neighbouring village, leaving Sumati on her own in that weak condition.

He reached on the bank of river Ganga after three hours of a road trip on a bullock cart. A journey slightly more than an hour in the mighty waters of Ganga followed by a couple of hours of road trip further to the neighbouring village remained. Vyas and few other commuters hired a boatman and stepped into the boat which had a mast and sails.

It was late evening, and total darkness prevailed in a few minutes. The temperature dipped down suddenly. Thick layers of mists and clouds gulped the night sky. Stars seemed stricken by the thunderheads. The stormy winds emerged to push the still waters to rough, which transformed into heaps of irate waves. Suddenly, the calm, serene water of the Ganges baffled out with great rage. The moon was throwing down shudders of light with a spooky sparkle. Underneath the moon, the rain moved towards Vyas like an apparition's cover of distress. A winnowing wind aged and moaned, undulating the surface of the carcass quiet Ganga. The boatman and his assistant tried to adjust the mast and get the sails down and to tie them off. They slipped on the downpour of the splashed deck. Commuters froze to see the panic on the boatman's face. The violent winds hammered the raindrops into their faces like small stones pricking them and pushed their hoods back. The boat squeezed, first up waves at forty-five degrees, and after that slammed down shaking their bones. At a certain point, the waves spun the vessel sideways. They held firmly onto the pole, onto ropes, onto anything. Holding tight was hard. Vyas, for the first time, felt his own mortality. The icy cold water of the Ganges lashed his face several times, and he felt a fever in his eyes. He knew it was going to be a rough and unpleasant passage. Seemed as if Ganga promised hardship and story of recoveries for anybody that would make it out with their skin that night.

Realising that he is in deep trouble and stranded away from his home and wife, Vyas pondered upon his decision to come for the seeds. After a while, the storm subsided. Rain, clouds and stormy winds were gone, and moonlight, stars and tranquil water of Ganga appeared. As if nature, trolled Vyas just like that! What made him even upset were evil and negative thoughts that arose in his mind after witnessing the aggressive rage of the Ganges. He worried about the events which would occur in the future. 'Sure enough, something serious is going to happen soon.

Mother nature has indicated to me such,' he thought looking up at the sky.

Sumati waited for her husband for the entire day, but he didn't come to her. She went to bed, hunching that Vyas would return on the next day only. There, Vyas reached *Sarpanch's* house in that village and told him the reason for the visit and that he was stuck in the storm in the river. *Sarpanch* was aware of the stormy weather, responding in agreement with Vyas and offered him food and shelter in the house. Certainly, that was not the first-time Vyas visited that village. Every notable person in the neighbouring village knew him very well. After a while, Vyas expressed his desire to sleep as he wanted to collect the seeds from the market and leave early in the morning for his home.

Sarpanch made two beddings for Vyas and himself on the open-air veranda of his house. Both laid on their beds, gazing at stars twinkling in the night sky. The mercury light of the moon was brightening up that patio with a sharp glow. As if moonlight tried reminding Vyas of something of grave importance. Thinking about the condition of Sumati at home, he decided to get up as early as possible the next day. He planned on collecting the seeds from the market and leaving for his village early in the morning. His eyes felt the weight of exhaustion he went through that day and slightly closed.

"What a beautiful complete moon, perfectly round in shape glittering in the night sky, Vyas!" said *Sarpanch*.

"Amazing indeed, *Sarpanch Ji*," Vyas responded calmly.

"May this night of the full moon bring prosperity to our lives," *Sarpanch* made a turn in his bed while commenting so.

'On the night of the next full moon, Sumati will give birth to a divine child. It will be a baby boy...' in a fraction of a second it echoed with a bang inside Vyas's mind, and he almost had all of his faculties collapsed.

'What have I done? Oh, Lord!' he got up from the bed in a snap and was not in a condition to say anything. He was stunned, slightly froze for few moments. *Sarpanch* panicked after seeing Vyas struck with hysteria. He never saw Vyas losing his calm and peace in an instant. Upon asking, Vyas told him that per the prediction of *Maha-Purohit*, Sumati would give birth to his child on that very night of the full moon. He suddenly stood up, preparing himself to leave immediately.

"Late night departures would not be possible, Vyas," said *Sarpanch*, further suggesting, "Ganga will not get any sailor until dawn. You must leave tomorrow morning."

Vyas was distraught, unable to figure out any way to speak to Sumati. Entrapped in vigorous nervousness, he muttered, "She will be in what condition? Where would she be? What if *Maha-Purohit* was right? I did so wrong by leaving her alone. Oh! What have I done?" He sweated profusely and trembled uncontrollably.

Sarpanch made him sit and offered a glass of water. That silent calming night shaped itself to be a nightmare for Vyas and his family as the universe spanned its wings of wrath upon few good people left on the face of the earth.

There Sumati, after midnight felt the early labour pains, realising that the time of the month had come when *Maha-Purohit* predicted the birth of her child. Her focus on the night of full moon was out until that moment. She was anxious, thrilled, excited, afraid, happy, sad, worried, in pain, hopeful, grateful, vulnerable and vigorous at the same time. Somehow, she got up from her bed and reached to the house of an elderly *Amma* next door, knocking on the door until *Amma* came out a few seconds later.

Sumati sweated profusely, and she fell on the doorstep unconsciously. *Amma* knew her condition, and she called to all the women around. Sumati was taken in the field and laid down on the ground. That peacefully stirring silent night suddenly mired in turbulence created by the movements of women roaming here and there in search of anything that could help *Amma* deliver Sumati's child. All the families in that village were aware of the childbirth and were eager to see the miraculous baby.

In a situation of absence of resources and proper medical help in the community, few experienced women including *Amma* performed that responsible task of assisting a mother in delivering her child. A temporary camp was soon set up using clothes like sari, suit, dupatta and bed sheets. Men vacated that place immediately but stood a little far away from the camp. Sumati writhed in immense pain as some women started getting the baby out. Her cry pierced the darkness of hollow night and travelled as far as it could. Everything went well as expected and shortly after the child was born, his first cry was heard all over the place. Everyone greeted each other and gathered around the camp. Sumati was soaked in sweat, lying numb and exhausted on the ground. Her voice was completely shut down, and she stopped moving at all. Some concerned women brought that into *Amma*'s notice. She then suggested that it was normal for some mothers to lie unconsciously due to the intense amount of energy exhausted in the delivery process. The child was handed over to another woman standing nearby who cleaned the baby and tucked him in a silky cloth. Eklavya's face looked sharp and was puffed merrily. After all, the scion of Ikshvaku had the power to change the world.

People embraced that night of the full moon. Suddenly, a huffing wind ascended then, blending the folds of that tent. A tinkling sound went to their ears as the first drops of rain fell onto the leaves. The sound resembled the rough clunking of glass, lilting and bright. A sheet of rain passed by them and the noise increased. The commotion on the tent resembled the phut-phut-phut as the hails make when they hit the ground. This sudden dramatic change in the weather took everyone by surprise. It wasn't the delicate, soaked, swollen drops of spring they were hearing; it resembled as if hard stones were hitting the canvas rooftop with unleashed power. They all could likewise listen to a periodic kerplunking sound. It was brought on by the water accumulated on the tent tumbling to the ground in a large swash of discharge. The moon was now hidden behind the thick black wall of clouds. The temperature decreased as they all crouched together and shuddered in the tent. For a brief minute, they imagined that they may be bound travellers, bound to escape in a powerful surge. Sumati was lying asleep, still weak and quiet. Now *Amma* worried about her. Sumati, after being nudged by those women several times, did not open her eyes. *Amma* shouted for some water. Everyone panicked, but Eklavya was utterly silent. The innocent child had no idea about what was going on there. *Amma* checked Sumati's heartbeat and breath.

"Hey, Ram!" she wailed and was in tears. All the villagers knew what had happened. Sumati was lying dead. She left for her heavenly abode soon after giving birth to Eklavya. The atmosphere of happiness and celebration soon turned into the tragic and fearful night of mourning.

Figure: Farewell forever - Sumati lying dead on the ground.

3: The Final Goodbye

VYAS

I could not even think of sleeping that night at *Sarpanch's* house, desperately waiting for the dawn to prosper. It seemed to me that the dark of the night took many days to retreat. And as soon as the first chirp of the birds fell into my ears, I left that house and quickly purchased the seeds from the market while proceeding towards the banks of the Ganges. My mind discomforted with random thoughts, and steps became as swift as the blowing wind. I was able to take the very first boat sailing to my village.

There were very few people on that vessel and Ganga was calm as usual. After some time, I saw other passengers onboard gathering on one side of the deck, all looking in the same direction. Curious by their strange action, I decided to look at whatever they were looking at and saw a dead body drifting in the waters of the Ganges. It appeared twice of its size due to excessive inflammation. The scene was quite upsetting as the corpse was partially eaten by crocodiles in the river. We were then told by the boatman about the sinking of a canoe in the storm which occurred last night, causing the death of everybody onboard. I thanked Almighty for saving my life from that ghostly storm and prayed for the peaceful abode of departed souls.

'There must be a reason behind me being able to escape that wrath of the Ganges. What it could possibly be?' I wondered. After about an hour of the journey in that boat, I reached the bank of river Ganga even before the complete sunrise. Then I sat on a bullock cart that was of a rider from my village. He, after seeing expressions of concern on my face asked the reason behind that. I shared with him what all happened in the recent past only to get consolation and wishes for a happy and prosperous future of Eklavya in return. He also told me about the destruction caused by the flood last night. We both finally entered the village.

Everything was devastated, farming fields submerged in flood water, and all crops were destroyed by the wrath of the Ganges. Shelters and houses in the outer area collapsed, leaving a significant chunk of the population homeless and jobless. This was something that never happened in the past. However, I didn't have much time and focus on thinking upon it.

I was now excited and nervous at the same time. My mind filled with questions and expectations that almost made me run after getting off from that cart and minutes later, I reached into my neighbourhood. Upon arriving there, I felt something unearthly and weird as the streets were empty. All I could hear was the dragging sound of tree leaves on deserted roads. As if the entire village was gone depopulated, abandoned by its people. I felt a weird sensation, and my heart pounded heavily. My speed became too slow after I saw a child running towards me,

innocently shouting my name. Those few seconds turned
into years to me. The child asked me to follow him. We
walked rapidly, and I asked about the situation from the
kid but miserably failed to understand what he tried to
explain in his slurring words. He was too innocent to
understand and tell what happened last night. The crowd
saw me coming, and I saw them gathered in the field near
Amma's house.

After tussling for the whole night with the grieving
tapestry of Sumati's death, all the villagers were now quiet
and tired. Their dry eyes developed swelling, and their
faces looked numb. Seemed as if the bitter reality of death
defeated the intensity of their tears holding tremendous
grief in them. Everybody moved, making room for me so
that I could go to the centre of the crowd-circle. I rapidly
drove forward and saw Sumati lying down hemmed in
between the grass and draped in white sheets.

"Oh, God!" I muttered in sheer distress. Being not
able to think properly, I looked helplessly at Amma to
confirm if my wife was really dead. Amma nodded her
head and cried again vigorously. I fell on the ground
almost unconsciously, and then I mustered all my hope and
strength and started waking up my wife from her eternal
sleep. I wasn't ready to accept the reality and refused to
believe in Sumati's death. Some people separated me from
the corpse. I once again, fell on the ground lamenting. The
entire village plunged into intense mourning, slowly and
then all at once.

Even the creator himself must accept what destiny holds in its hands. I was just an ordinary man; how could I mould my fate? Somehow after bringing myself into consciousness, I with the help of the villagers made necessary arrangements for the funeral. Three other men picked up Sumati's bier with me. Her dead body was hefty. As if she did not want to leave me, Eklavya, her house and village even after her physical demise.

'Ram naam satya hai... satya hai, satya hai...' (the name of Ram is the truth) was chanted by the people following me on their way to the crematorium. Whoever on the way, saw the final journey of Sumati, folded their hands and prayed for her peaceful abode.

Human life is shattered under the influence of ego. It becomes difficult for us to do charity and give proper respect to the people around us. But man forgets that he needs the support of fellow people even after death. Why so ignorant then? Why so much hatred? Where is the love?

'Blessed are these three noble souls who are shouldering the bier of Sumati with me,' I thought and continued walking. 'Now I understand why Almighty saved me from that deadly storm last night. I have to live for Eklavya,' I further pondered. After a while, we arrived at the crematorium. That vast cemetery built on the banks of mighty Ganges conveyed and reflected the reality of life in the world which, under the influence of *Kali Yuga*, was lost in its own madness and material aspects.

Right after the entrance of the cemetery, lied a rock which had '*Antim Dham*' written over it. On that rock was a massive statue of Lord Shiva lost profoundly into the *samadhi*. The Lord of destruction himself stayed very calm in that cemetery. I felt as if *shamshan*, the place which offers a state of tranquillity to Lord Shiva and is better known for welcoming the dead, induces the life needed for the journey to a different heavenly world. Priests chanted Gayatri Mantra, and I under the supervision of *Maha-Purohit* performed all funeral rituals for Sumati, my better half, preferably the best one.

Villagers departed for their homes after some time, but I cared less and stood still, plunged deep into my thoughts and staring at ginormous fire blazing out of Sumati's deathbed. Seeing me struggling with that unfortunate situation perhaps filled *Amma*'s heart with compassion, and she took responsibility for nurturing Eklavya until he becomes wise enough to face the wrath of the world. *Amma* was a motherly figure to me, and I had no doubts about her upbringing. So I agreed with an expression of regard and compliance to her for that significant step taken to help my family in its difficult times.

The deathbed completely vanished after a few hours. What remained was a pile of ash with some red-hot chunks of wood scattered all over. Sumati's body was taken over by holy fire, leaving behind few of her bones, partly burnt and grey in colour. We went for our homes that evening, and next morning soon after sunrise, I visited the *shamshan* to collect those remains and poured it into the holy river, Ganga. That act as per *Maha-Purohit* ensured my wife's safe departure to the heavens.

Nonetheless, it was I who wanted her soul to rest in peace wherever it was. I couldn't do much for her when she was with me, but I wanted to do everything that made her life easy in another world.

4: A Feeling of Loss

VYAS

It has been rightly said that the only constant in this world is the change itself. Thirteen years had passed, and life was back on track for Eklavya and me. I could never do away with my past, but I wasn't lost in the grieving memories of Sumati anymore. Though it took many years for me to get over the trauma I felt after losing my wife, yet I had understood that life goes on no matter what. On the other hand, Eklavya only imagined about his mother as he was too little when Sumati passed away. It was *Amma* who nurtured him like a mother for those thirteen years.

Eklavya became sensible and focused under *Amma*'s supervision. While I would often be busy in the farming and agricultural activities, *Amma* started Eklavya's home-schooling at an early age to make him confident. Besides studies, my son showed a keen interest in sports, and outdoor activities form a very young age. He often played with my farming equipment and used them as weapons in his games.

With the passage of time, Eklavya became mature enough to take care of himself, and it was time for him to attend formal schooling. Rudraputra had very few *Gurukul*s that had some influential and eminent teachers who made sure the quality of teaching remains uncompromised. Admission was granted after a short question-answer session between student and teacher. Teachers did so to check the aptitude standards of the child. There was no compulsory fee for children to earn their education in *Gurukul*s. Whatever parents gave, be it money, clothes, food or anything else was accepted happily and fully utilised. People in Rudraputra were very focused and grave about child education. Studying and acquiring knowledge in the *Gurukul*s was an essential aspect of life. On the other hand, gurus were always ready to help children and anybody for that matter. It was their dharma as *Brahmins* to impart knowledge in the society which they lived in and that too without expecting any economic benefits in return.

But things changed rapidly outside of the village. The vicious outbreak of *Kali Yuga* forced knowledge centres to charge a massive fee to the students. The education sector clamped with corruption made teaching merely a business. Gurus and *Acharya*s expressed interest in the money in exchange for knowledge, making acquiring and imparting of knowledge a dirty game of reaping benefits. Those who paid more got easy admission and particular attention. Helplessness bore the brunt of poor but promising students.

Luckily, my son got admitted to one of the *Gurukul*s that stood at the top of a mountain in the far outskirts of our village and was among the first established *mathas* by Adi Shankaracharya, the great philosopher and theologian. Those were the times when students left their homes and lived in the *Gurukul* as it wasn't possible for them to commute daily. *Gurukul*s were generally established in the outskirts of town or village to keep the environment free from any civil disturbance. It represented a school cum hostel model of education. Eklavya prepared himself to leave his home for *Gurukul*.

As a child, he was quite sad to leave behind *Amma* and me, but he was mature enough to understand the importance of education and moved gracefully. The fact that he would learn martial arts along with other subjects made him excited about going there. *Amma* and I bid farewell to him with a heavy heart. We knew it will not be possible for us to visit his *Gurukul* as there was only one chariot service that took visitors and parents uphill once in three months. Moreover, that service was expensive. Our immense love for Eklavya made it hard for us to imagine our lives for a few years without him being around. Probably we loved him more than he loved us. Love is contagious, and so are its side-effects. I had no clue that this separation from him would trigger a series of unfortunate events in my life.

Amma remained depressed for a few days after Eklavya left her. I made every possible effort to pull her out from that state of trauma but could not succeed. Even more, I needed someone to divert my mind from worrying about my son. *Amma* might have thought that I never knew about her crying in disguise, but I could sense her low spirits from time to time. We both miserably missed Eklavya. The wall that held our emotions and made us strong just… collapsed. Initially, I thought *Amma* was just sad, but things got worse when she began losing her consciousness quite often. She frequently blabbered something, acted weird, coughed and vomited. Local *Vaidya* was called, and after carefully assessing *Amma*'s condition gave me some herbs for her. I gave those herbs as directed by the *Vaidya* but saw no progress in her condition. Albeit, those herbs caused more harm to her health. After a few days, she developed severe pain in her entire body. I had to quit my work to take good care of her and eventually, I ran out of money. Seeing me in this situation, some villagers helped me with *Amma*'s medications. Even that did not last long, and she showed no improvement in her health.

She was somehow aware of the difficulties and trouble I faced because of her. Being ashamed and sorry for causing problems to me, she begged to God for her death. *Amma*'s pain was so immense that she wished to be murdered. She often cried and shouted at me, asking me to kill her, suggesting different ways of ending her life. She demanded to get killed by mixing poison in her food. I just could not do anything but listen to her and let everything go. She lost her sanity entirely, and she shouted and cried out of her pain, each night. I, on the other hand, always tried to give her some medicinal herbs prescribed by the *Vaidya* but failed each time. Those herbs didn't do any good to her. Also, it became hard for me to feed those medicines to *Amma*. She fell asleep for a few hours under the influence of those drugs and then she again continued to shout and blabber. That tragic situation went on for some days. At times, she cursed *Maha-Purohit* and blamed him for plotting behind Sumati's death. I, however, never cared about what *Amma* claimed as she lost her ability to think correctly. Seeing her suffering from immense pain, having no money to support us both, and having nobody to take care of the situation gradually turned me into a dead soul trapped in a body of flesh and blood.

It was about two months since Eklavya left the village. One night, I did not hear anything from *Amma* for hours. I checked if everything was alright, sneaking into her room and saw her lying on the bed with eyes closed. She exhausted utterly and sweated a lot.

'Probably, she is still under the medicinal effect,' I thought and left quietly. I had not slept properly in the last couple of weeks, and I wanted to sleep for a thousand years. I didn't know when I fell asleep that night.

The first thing I did after waking up the next morning was to rush to *Amma*'s room. What I saw there completely shattered me. She laid peacefully in her bed with her eyes closed. Her stomach did not rise and fall, and her limbs stretched weirdly. Though I had a hunch of what had happened, I still went closer and gave her few nudges to wake her up. I placed my hand on her chest that contained a dead heart. Her body was cold. So cold. *Amma* was in her eternal sleep. She was lying dead, and I realised that soon. All her sufferance and pain vanished, and she was now safe from the perils of this world. I saw too much suffering and pain of *Amma* and underwent immense emotional and mental distress, so much so that her death seemed vibrant to me. I had no sentimentality left for that death. I sat beside the dead body, and tears started pouring down my eyes. *Amma*'s wish was heard, she was freed forever from her pain.

I, no matter how desperate and helpless I was, could not call my son at that time of great grief. Eklavya was too far, and that mountain was impassable to anybody unless they are on that chariot explicitly designed for the trek. Unfortunately, there still was a month left in the return of that chariot service. Eklavya's presence was required, but there was no way I could keep *Amma*'s body for that long, and so, I cremated it without my son. Life kept on flinging jibes after jibes at me until I couldn't bear it anymore.

5: The Debate

TIME

The map of spiritual India in the ninth century was substantially shaped by Adi Shankaracharya and his followers. Establishment of *mathas* across the subcontinent ensured proper propagation of *Advaita Vedanta* among the youth. Predictions of *Maha-Purohit* began taking shape as Eklavya developed an interest in learning theology and war skills. He, however, was unaware of those prophecies made about him about fourteen years ago.

EKLAVYA

I gradually settled down in the serene environment of my *Gurukul* and was far beyond the clutches of the worldly perils. The *Gurukul* was established by Adi Shankaracharya and was known for its teachings of theology and combat skills. Students from all corners of the country wanted admission there, but very few managed to get in. I was amazed at the complex and grand construction of *Gurukul* atop a mountain surrounded by lush greenery in the lap of mother nature. Students wake up a little bit before the sunrise and bathe. After that, *Acharyas* guided them to the prayer field. After morning prayer, all the *Acharyas* and students sat together and had their breakfast. Students would do the dishes afterwards and reached their classes in the same field they prayed in. That area served as an open-air classroom during the day and combat training centre during the evening. There were few halls in the building as well, but everybody preferred learning outside.

Students were taught one theory subject and one combat skill for each year spent in the *Gurukul*. Theory subjects were designed to strengthen the minds and decision-making skills of the pupils whereas, combat skills made them ready for the future complications they might face due to the rise of the *Kali*. The examination conducted at the end of the year where *Acharyas* gauged our abilities against the level of training we got.

I learned about self-control and importance of dharma from *Acharya* Bhushan or Bhushanacharya as other gurus called him. Bhushanacharya was responsible for teaching theory subjects to my batch for the first three years in the *Gurukul*. Whereas, it was *Acharya* Virbhadra's responsibility to train us in combat for the first three years spent there. *Acharya* Virbhadra was among the mightiest masters of war skills. Both Bhushanacharya and *Acharya* Virbhadra were once disciples of Adi Shankaracharya.

I cultivated a positive influence on most of my classmates and *Acharya*s in the *Gurukul* during the first year of study, passed my theory subject of self-control and importance of dharma with flying colours, and defeated Pundir in archery and got promoted to the second year. Pundir was my best friend in the *Gurukul*. Both of us had similar interests in subjects and combating. Pundir came from a nearby village situated on the other side of the mountain. He was always concerned about his family back home as his village was often raided by hill bandits. He wanted to learn as many combating skills as he could and teach his villagers how to fight to get rid of the atrocities they faced because of those hooligans.

Though most of the *Gurukul* was devoid of harmful elements, yet some students were jealous of my might. But that was least of my concerns at that time. What I was most worried about was the intention of *Acharya* Kaushal to stoop me down for anything and everything I did. Kaushalacharya kept an eye on my activities as he was primarily worried that I would soon surpass the degree of intellect his students had. Perhaps, he was clutched entirely into the grip of the evil.

During the second year of my study, everyone in the *Gurukul* acknowledged my dedication and hard work as a learner. All *Acharya*s were convinced of my perseverance and integrity. I had become a role model for my juniors and was given love and support from the seniors. I also participated in all volunteer works and often trained my juniors in archery. By the end of the second year, I became as perfect as anybody else in mixed martial arts, archery, theology and self-control and was the most favourite student of *Acharya* Bhushan and Virbhadra. I never knew what special I had in me that made almost everybody appreciate me there. Seeing me forging ahead with tremendous progress added fuel to Kaushalacharya's jealousy for me. He waited for the right time to challenge my understanding of spirituality and realising true self. I was the son of Vyas and the scion of Ikshvaku, how could I have let my father's and *Amma's* expectations fall short? And so, I prepared myself internally to face *Acharya* Kaushal in the future.

Days turned into weeks and weeks into months. Another year passed and my three years of tenure at *Gurukul* was near the end. Students could visit their families for a maximum of three months after undertaking three years of progressive education and training in the *Gurukul*. I eagerly waited for the final exams so that I could go visit my family. I often missed *Amma* while I was there. Mainly because of the food she prepared for me. Her food was way better than what they served to the students in *Gurukul*. The only thing other than food which bothered me was the teaching methodology of some *Acharya*s like Kaushalacharya. No student questioned him, ever. Whatever was taught by him to his students was taken as the final and last word. This kept the students from learning practically and killed their curiosity to know more. I was often told that I was way ahead of my classmates at the time of admission there. I often thanked *Amma* because she home-schooled me. I excitedly imagined how Father would feel upon seeing me excelling in all those subjects and skills.

Soon the day arrived when I had to take my theory and practical exam. A consortium of *Acharya*s was set up to examine the students as usual. I was called upon the platform and asked to show the combating skills in sword fighting, a skill that I mastered during the third year of my training from *Acharya* Virbhadra. After displaying few moves I had learnt, a senior was called to fight with me. I fought with whatever I had learned from *Acharya* and won the fight without much of a tussle. The moment *Acharya* Virbhadra was about to declare the results in combating, Kaushalacharya intervened. He demanded that I must be tested for other fighting skills in archery and mixed martial arts as well. In my heart of hearts, I was prepared for something like this as I knew *Acharya* Kaushal was also a part of the consortium. I fought with the opponent in martial arts and showed some classic shots with my bow and arrow. The results were even better than what they were in previous years. Everybody applauded except for Kaushalacharya. I was declared pass in the combating skills examination.

Archery was in my blood. Not that Father was an archer, but I got the hang of it quickly in the *Gurukul*. It was *Acharya* Virbhadra who first told me that Eklavya is someone who learns, and masters bow and arrow. I never thought my name would have a meaning to it.

After having lunch, the consortium gathered again for my theory examination. *Acharya* Bhushan asked me some questions that were quickly and aptly answered. Now it was sure that I would be promoted to the fourth year and allowed to visit my village for three months before commencing further study and training.

"That would be all, Eklavya. I declare you pass in my..." Bhushanacharya ended his sentence mid-way after he saw Kaushalacharya coming towards the platform. I knew I had to face the wrath of *Acharya* Kaushal developed from the jealousy that he accumulated for the last three years.

"I will take his test. If he passes, we will let him go to his village," Kaushalacharya said. It was one of the rarest events in the history of *Gurukul* when someone who did not teach the student took the test of that student, yet everybody agreed out of courtesy. Moreover, other *Acharya*s were confident that I would pass the spiritual debate I was about to have with Kaushalacharya.

"What is *asatya*?" he began.

"All that is visible...everything that is noticeable and experienced by all is *asatya*," I replied.

"With all due respect, *Acharya* Kaushal what you just asked was from a higher course that has not yet been taught to Eklavya," argued Bhushanacharya.

"That should not be your concern, *Acharya*. I want to see how much this scion of Ikshvaku knows about his true-self," counter-argued Kaushalacharya and bombarded a series of tough and complicated questions.

"What is the meaning of 'all that is visible'?" asked *Acharya*.

"Whatever is visible and obvious, whatever is the object of the mind and the senses," I continued, "And what I know personally that alone is visible. What I know actually that by itself is visible."

"Who knows the seer? Who sees the self?"

"No one's help is required to see the self, just the way the sun does not need a lamp for light. It is self-illuminating," I replied confidently.

"Where has this world come from and how?"

"This world has originated from Him and Him alone."

"Who is He?" *Acharya* asked while raising one of his eyebrows. He seemed to be pretty sure I would fail to answer that question.

"He is the Ultimate Being, He is the Supreme Ruler. He is the one who creates the world with His illusory power. He alone is the creator, the sustainer and the destroyer of this world," I replied with my head held high.

"How does *Brahman* create, sustain and destroy this world?" another tough question.

"The way a spider spins its web, moves about in it and later on swallows it. Similarly, God creates, sustains and destroys the world." Another simple answer from my side.

"What is *jiva*?"

"*Jiva* is the soul, and despite the fact it is changeless, under the influence of spiritual ignorance it mistakenly starts considering itself to be the mind and the body. What's more, that is the reason why it experiences the world."

"What is *Avidya*?" *Acharya* Kaushal became hyper.

"Considering not-self to be the self, considering the changeless as variable, and considering this world to be real is *avidya*." I was at ease but wondered about how that debate was going to end.

"Then what is *Vidya*?"

"The knowledge of the self is *Vidya*. '*Sa Vidya Ya Vimuktaye*'. *Vidya* is what liberates us from all sorrows, clashes, pain, bondage, conflicts, servitude, illusions and fantasies. *Vidya* is that which frees us from the feeling of duality, the idea that we are two individual entities, the idea that we are separate, and that 'You' and 'I' are different. *Vidya* gives the insight with which one can perceive one's nature as *Brahman*." Everyone looked stunned to hear that reply coming from me.

"What is the process of realising *Brahman*?" Kaushalacharya was almost shouting at me now.

"There are two ways to acknowledge *Brahman*. The first way is to know what *Brahman* is not. To exclude that which is not *Brahman*. After excluding all names, forms, qualities, flaws, variables, getting to know the one who is changeless. The second way is to recognise the truth just the way it is. It is of the nature of existence. Without it, the world has no existence at all. It was and is *Brahman*. That is the reason I am *Brahman*, you are *Brahman*, every one of us is *Brahman* alone. So, the entire world is *Brahman*."

"Brilliant!" *Acharya* Bhushan cheered and perhaps felt proud of me.

"How can one know *Brahman*?" *Acharya* Kaushal was supplanted with anger.

"*Brahman* can be known by righteous social life, spiritual reflection, listening attentively, pondering over daily experiences, contemplating upon inferences and by entering into *samadhi*," I answered politely.

"What are the traits of *Brahma-Gyani*?"

There was a silence all over after Kaushalacharya asked this question. No student gave an appropriate answer to this question in the history of religious debates of the *Gurukul*. I bent my head down in introspection. There was a devil's smile on Kaushalacharya's face, and other *Acharya*s were sympathising with *Acharya* Bhushan. And then...

"If anyone asserts that he has realised *Brahman*, at the point really he has not acknowledged *Brahman*. As soon as one realises *Brahman*, the conceit of having realised *Brahman* vanishes," I replied, my voice as serene as fine droplets falling from a cloudless sky after sunset.

"Splendid! Brilliant! Splendid!" everybody appreciated my glaring intellect. Perhaps, my inner quest of finding true-self and God was evident from the answers I gave. *Acharya* Kaushal retreated in shame. An exemplary warrior and theologian was born inside me that day. I was given permission to visit my family in the village.

Figure: Acharya Kaushal and Eklavya debating.

6: Unwelcome Home

TIME

After spending three years in the *Gurukul* and learning about self-control, character development, the importance of dharma and propagation of internal and external purity, 16-years-old Eklavya could visit his family for three months. He was delighted to go back to his village and to see his family. He became even wiser and more mature than what he was three years ago. He packed his stuff and collected all his achievement certificates to show his father and fellow villagers. He couldn't sleep that night as he thought about the glorious upcoming day. Next morning, the chariot was called to the *Gurukul* and those who wanted to go downhill sat in it. After some time, they all reached down the hill and got off the. The chariot then picked up those who waited to go uphill and climbed up.

After a few hours of ride on a bullock cart, Eklavya arrived at his village. Everything seemed normal in the community. He met few known passers-by while on his way to the village. Little did he know that he was going to witness a life-changing experience which would turn everything upside down in his happy, easy-going life.

Upon reaching the house, he held the handle of the main door and found it already open to his surprise. The wooden door that became slightly off colour from the walls loomed over him. For a second, Eklavya could vividly picture his childhood spent in that house. He did not see anyone inside. Surprised by the sudden absence of his father and *Amma*, he looked for them restlessly. The house was covered in a thick grey layer of dust and had spider webs on the walls. The bricks and wood were damp and cold as if it were turning dead. *Amma*'s room had water seeping in through the window. Brown furs indicated the presence of rats in the house.

'How long had it been since *Amma* and Father left it?' he thought and ran outside, searching nearby streets and backyard but could not locate either of them. Finally, he knocked on the neighbour's door. Someone opened the door, and they closed it immediately upon the sight of him. Nobody let Eklavya inside their house. In fact, nobody saw him for more than a moment, making him feel incredibly awkward. Those who were fond of him, pampered him, those who played along, took good care of him suddenly refused to acknowledge his presence, leave alone talking and welcoming. After trying his best to ask every known person about his family and eventually failing to get an answer, Eklavya sat down on the ground with his heart heavy and mind loaded with questions and anxiety.

After some time, he saw *Maha-Purohit* passing through a street nearby. It was an optimistic moment for Eklavya as he was filled with sudden joy and ran towards *Maha-Purohit*, shouting and requesting him to stop. *Maha-Purohit* was equally ignorant as other villagers, but he could not resist a child's request and stopped for Eklavya.

Upon asking about his family, Eklavya got no response from *Maha-Purohit*.

"Where is *Amma*? Have you seen my father??" he asked in worrying tone but got no reply. The silence of *Maha-Purohit* gave even worse feeling to Eklavya. Someone who always supported him and guided him and his family suddenly acted as if he never knew him. Eklavya could not hold his frustration and fear, and he cried vigorously. *Maha-Purohit* then made him sit on the ground and said,

"*Amma* died after two months of your departure to *Gurukul*." Eklavya stopped crying suddenly and looked at *Maha-Purohit* with his eyes wide open. Before he said anything further, *Maha-Purohit* continued again.

"For the first time in my life, I witnessed my predictions and calculations gone wrong completely. You are indeed unholy and sullied for the entire village and the Ikshvaku clan! The day before your birth, *Mata* Ganga showed us her rage. There was a storm, and many people died. Our crops and fields were devastated completely by flood; people became homeless and jobless. You brought an endless misfortune for all of us. However, we all were busy celebrating your birth and overlooked what was going on. It was you who took the life of your own mother. Sumati, your mother died just after your birth. It took thirteen years for Vyas to recover from that unfortunate event. And now, *Amma* died a painful death because of you. She grieved with your memories. After all that, your father Vyas lost his sanity and consciousness. He became mentally unsound and even posed a threat to our lives. You shall find him roaming the streets anytime soon. All of this because of you! You are a cursed child, Eklavya. You are sullied! Whoever came close and became important in your life was devastated, completely! That is why, we all have decided to do away with you, we all have chosen to abandon you as our child. Nobody in this village will recognise you as an Ikshvaku. We cease to acknowledge you! It's better for you to depart from here and leave this community. Let people live their lives without fearing your unholy presence. Don't come back here, ever!" *Maha-Purohit* left immediately after that.

Eklavya could not get his head around what *Maha-Purohit* just said. He could not believe that he was deemed cursed and sullied by his own people. While he pondered upon what went wrong in those three years and even before his birth, he saw a barefoot man wrapped in a dirty cloth, wearing torn dhoti, having long hair and beard standing near him, staring continuously. Being uncomfortable by the offensive presence of that man, Eklavya shouted,

"Now what do you want from me? Go away!" The man smiled and pointed his finger towards Eklavya. Eklavya was about to fall on the ground, his knees unable to carry his own weight after he realised that the man standing in front of him was no other than Vyas, his father. Eklavya touched Vyas's feet and hugged him tightly. He cried profusely. Vyas, on the other hand, could not bless his son. He was almost unaware of what was going on there.

"What happened to you, father? How did *Amma* die?? Why they are not talking to me, letting me in, why! Am I cursed, father?? Did I murder my mother? Speak up!!" Eklavya bombarded a series of endless questions. However, all Vyas did was standing still with his head bent down.

Figure: Eklavya knocking doors in the neighbourhood, only to get disregard in return.

7: A Worthy Vivification

TIME

That day held exceptional importance in Eklavya's life as he lost everyone but discovered himself. He didn't know how to leave his own village but knew where to go, he had no clue about how he would live his life but was feeling alive, he was helpless yet robust enough to get going. It was then when he decided to leave his village, Vyas and everything else forever. He feared that his presence brought misfortune to the village and that Vyas could die of his cursed influence. He decided to go entirely out of reach of everyone he knew. All Eklavya had to himself were the memories, both good and evil, of his past and the teachings of the elders. It was time for him to put to work all the theories he learned from *Acharya* Bhushan. Eklavya decided of not going back to the *Gurukul* as it would be too late for him to discover his true self. With all that, his journey began, filled with courage and optimism to seek the truth and God.

His inner quest to find the truth about God was at stake and he would not let it go so quickly. He proceeded to the north towards the Himalayas. It was a tough decision for Eklavya but was totally worth the pain. He awakened spiritually, he was adamant to understand the cycle of life and looked to find answers to some of the most critical questions of his life. Other teenagers of his age desired of playing with friends, studying, eating delicious food, to be acknowledged and get importance whereas, Eklavya wished for nothing materialistic and as he gained higher consciousness, his perspective about everything in this Universe changed dramatically.

EKLAVYA

I travelled on foot and after a few hours, reached the shore of the river Ganga which was in the north direction. The span of the river was narrower at that point as compared to what it was near the village in the south. Instead of waiting for a ferry to arrive and pick me up from the bank, I took a deep plunge into the cold water of the Ganges and started swimming. It took only a few minutes to cross the river and reach another side of it. I was tired, shivering in cold and hungry. I had no money, no clothes and nobody with me. I thought of returning to my village quite a few times but then reminded myself that it would not make any difference as I had no money and clothes there as well. Also, nobody in that village cared about me anymore. So I kept on going. At least no one was there to be afraid of my so-called unholy presence.

I think I was at war with my inner peace and harmony. It was too much for a vulnerable teenager to take on to. I realised that life is just a small fussy realm where nothing is predictable. Grumbling inside my mind about what destiny made me go through, I sat on the ground with my eyes wet with tears. Few minutes after crying, complaining about life in my own mind and blaming God for everything terrible occurred in my life, I had to do something to satisfy my hunger.

The land along the edge of Ganga was vast and devoid of any plantation. Few stalls sold some local fast food to the tourists and commuters. Few other people on the shore waited for their ferries, some of them washed clothes and bathe in the river. I could have begged those people for money, but my self-respect did not let me do so. After walking ahead for some time, I saw a bunch of children taking continuous dives into the water and coming out with something bright and shiny inside their mouths. I took a closer look and saw those children spitting coins out of their mouths and counting it with delight. People including locals and seasonal tourists often threw some coins in the holy river and made a wish. Nobody knows if their dreams ever come true by doing that. However, this act of them provided poor children with an opportunity to get that money and buy their food almost daily. I was full of joy after seeing that as I decided to collect some coins for my meal. Diving into the deep cold water of Ganga seemed much more comfortable than begging for money.

After coming out of the Ganges with my mouth full of coins, I bought some food from nearby vendors and ate it religiously. Ganga gave good business to boatmen, food vendors and to those children who collected money from inside it. Even though my hunger was taken care of, my mental stress continuously arose. I knew the sole purpose of my life of finding and realising true-self and of knowing the creator but didn't know how to do that. With no hope and courage left in my mind, I suddenly recalled all the painful and unfortunate events that occurred in the past, blaming myself for Maa's death, *Amma*'s suffering and painful death, Father's devastating mental condition and everything my villagers went through 'supposedly' because of my cursed influence. Tormented with immense pain and agony, I thought to end my life by taking *samadhi* into Ganga. Death seemed to be the end of my suffering. I stood up and walked towards the river. While covering the distance between me and the river, all I saw was a ginormous mass of water that could have quickly gulped anything that came close to it.

"I am lost! Could you please help me find my way?" I heard a loud voice from behind and stopped to look back. A tall man with a small bag stood a little far behind me.

"Go ask someone else for help. I am going to end my life right here, right now! Don't distract me..." I responded annoyingly and continued walking towards the river.

"I think we are going to meet again after you are dead. Burial or fire, what do you want me to do with your body?" he replied instantaneously. His question seemed interestingly weird and made me bound to stop walking and think about its answer.

"What do you mean we are going to meet after I die?" I asked thoughtfully while coming back to where he was standing.

"My father manages a cemetery built on the other side of the river. He is getting older and too weak to do any work there. That is why he asked me to take over his role. I am coming from the holy city of Banaras after completing my higher studies from a *Gurukul* there. Now that I will work in that cemetery, I am sure I will perform the last rites of your unclaimed body after you die. Thus, I said we will meet again after your death. I never got a chance to ask a dead person about how they liked to be cremated. So I did not want to lose this opportunity to ask an about-to-be dead person about how he would like to be cremated," explained that man with humour. I smiled gently after hearing his reply. The impulse and rage with which I proceeded towards the river to end my life without thinking wisely vanished in a moment.

"I was much younger than you when I left my home. I don't remember the shortest route to the cemetery, and now I think I am lost," further said the man.

"The cemetery you are going to work at is on the outskirts of my village on the other side of the river. I have never been there, but I can tell it would take you less than an hour to reach there on foot. You should take that ferry and reach the other shore first," I suggested while pointing out a ferry.

"What about you, aren't you coming? Didn't you just say it is your village on the other side of the river?" he questioned.

"I left my village forever. People there are afraid of my so-called unholy existence. Nobody loves me, nobody cares for me as they did before. They say I killed my mother right after my birth. *Amma...* died because of me. My father lost his sanity and is mentally unsound now. I left him as I was afraid he would die of my unholy presence. Nobody talked to me there. They deem me as a cursed child. I must not go there!" replied I in a frustrated voice.

"That's sad, I am sorry. Why don't you come work with me in the cemetery? It's not inside your village. Nobody knows you there," he made an offer.

"I will go to the north towards the Himalayas for my *sadhana*," I said with a firm tone, thinking it would deflect the topic of discussion.

"Oh dear! How would you reach there? And more importantly, what would you do there?" he said. I did not want to answer his questions, but then I realised I would be dead by then had he not asked the way to the cemetery. I at least owe him some answers, and so I said,

"I shall seek God and the truth of this life. I shall learn to live without taking any assistance from others, and I shall understand how the laws of karma make their course in *Kali Yuga*. The solitude would help me discover these things."

"I will not stop you from doing what you want to do. But you are still naïve to learn and explore the dimensions of life. Come work with me in the cemetery.

You were going to die anyway. Had I not asked you to help me with my way, you would be dead already! Let's take a closer look and understand the truth of death before you go ahead to the Himalayas to understand the lie of the life. What say?" asked the man, leaving me pondering upon what he just said. After thinking for a while, I agreed to go with him. We rushed to get on a small boat sailing towards the north and to the other side of the river.

Figure: Seeking fortune in the depths - Children diving into the Ganges to collect coins.

8: The Known Stranger

EKLAVYA

"I am Mohammad, by the way," he said.

"My name is Eklavya," I replied and couldn't keep myself from asking, "You are a Muslim, how come they let you study in the *Gurukul*?" with sheer surprise on my face.

He was quite shocked after listening to that question. Perhaps, seeing a young boy passing such strong comment was something unexpected to him. However, he seemed to be impressed with my tendency to ask uneasy and prompt questions.

"Everyone has the right to education, and under no circumstances, humans shall ever be discriminated by their religion, for it is the man who created religions and not contrariwise; this was their mission in the *Gurukul*", said Mohammad.

"What? Were you in Adi Shankaracharya's *matha* in Banaras?" I asked him. He nodded in affirmative and passed a smile. I was amazed at the coincidence of us both being the students of the *Gurukuls* that shared same ideologies.

"I still don't understand what made you leave your village permanently and most importantly, what made your mind about going to the Himalayas…" he continued questioning me.

"To seek God, I must detach myself from worldly aspirations. I must have a free mind and a pure soul. My village did not seem to be the right place for me to begin my quest. Therefore, I decided to move to the Himalayas, in absolute serenity, far away from this noisy world," I replied.

"You seem to have misinterpreted what they taught you in the *Gurukul.* You don't need to be out of this noisy world to seek Him; instead, get the noise inside you out! It does not matter where you live, rather, how and what you live to create the difference is the essence of life. Spending the rest of your life in solitude would not let you seek the complete truth. It will make you dull and weak with each passing day. You must embrace the euphoria of this beautiful life Almighty has given you. Make every moment count. Even Buddha realised after being in complete solitude for a few months that it is more important to calm the world which lives inside you than the world in which you live," he enlightened me.

"Do not tell me what to do, what not to do. It is I who decide what's best for me and not anybody else. Spending more time in the *Gurukul* does not make you any superior of the human beings. I will see what I will do." I could not control my emotions, and ego took over my mind.

"Allow me to tell you a story while we are on this ferry," Mohammad said and started without waiting for my approval.

"Once upon a time, there was a king who had a pet goat. That goat developed an uncontrolled appetite. No matter how much that goat ate, there was always some scope of hunger left in it. This annoyed the king. So, once he announced to give an enormous amount of money to anyone who would take that goat in the wilderness and feed lots of grass. He also kept one condition of determining if the stomach of the goat is full or not by performing a straightforward test of feeding the goat himself in the end. Listening to the announcement, a man came to the king and said that this task would be no big deal for him. He went to the jungle with that goat and set it free to move and graze. That goat kept on munching all day. After returning from the forest, that man claimed that goat fed all day and there was no way it could eat any more grass. As announced, the king was eager to perform the final test. As soon as he put some grass in front of that goat, it started eating it. The king stared at the man, and the man understood that he failed at that task. Similarly, many other citizens of the kingdom tried their best to satisfy the hunger of that goat but could not succeed as each time the king put some grass in front of that goat, it would start eating that.

One *Brahmin* scholar came to know about the announcement. He carefully thought about the situation and figured out a way to solve that mystery. He took that goat with him in the jungle. Every time that goat tried to eat some grass, that *Brahmin* would smash it with a wooden stick. He kept on doing so till the evening and did not let the goat eat anything. That goat developed a fear of getting smashed by a wooden stick upon eating any grass. In the evening, he returned to the court and claimed that he fed the goat to full capacity and that goat would not eat anything as it had its stomach full. The king was ready to test the hunger of that goat. He put some grass in front of that goat. That goat would not even come close to the grass, let alone eating it. The fear of being hit by wooden stick kept it under control. Everyone was surprised to see that. *Brahmin* earned his prize and left.

This goat is none other than your mind, Eklavya. The *Brahmin* who took that goat for grazing is *aatma*. That king represents the God (*param-aatma*). The mind, like that goat, will always try to graze more and more grass (material aspects). One should always keep their mind in control. This control would then improve their mind, body, heart and soul and ultimately enhance their lives. Often smash your thoughts with the wooden stick of your wisdom. This will not let your ego gain access to your mind. And then you will be ready to seek Him and experience His (God's) presence. Remember, decisions taken to calm your mind will not deliver in the long run. Instead, decisions made with the calm mind will benefit you for sure. Therefore, you should ease the world which is inside your mind and the world in which you live would become more serene ultimately."

Mohammad finished his story and looked at me with a thoughtful gaze. I, on the other hand, was wholly immersed in the story that made me realise that I should not let ego come in the way of my spiritual quest. Unable to control my emotions, I got tears in my eyes and hugged him.

"You are much like *Acharya* Bhushan," I said. Mohammad was skinny and tall, and maybe that was why I didn't really feel anything between my arms and the rest of the body when I hugged him.

"Pick up your stuff and be ready to disembark! Your trip ends here," shouted the sailor. There was a commotion on the deck. People lifted, pulled and pushed their luggage to get off from the ferry. We got off the vessel and continued our journey on foot until the cemetery arrived.

Figure: Brahmin taming the ever-grazing goat.

9: Life in the Land of the Dead

EKLAVYA

It was all gloomy that evening as the sun completely hid behind a thick layer of dark clouds under the horizon, leaving behind the dim and pale light of the sunlit half-moon. As Mohammad opened the rusty gates of the cemetery, a loud squeaky sound penetrated the silence spread all over the graveyard. Behind those gates lied the ocean of the dead, welcoming us to their barren kingdom. I felt a slight swoosh of cold air with the moist smell of soil and limestone in it.

The continuous chirping of grasshoppers and crickets was enough to set an unearthly fear inside my mind. Mohammad looked perfectly okay in that cemetery, it was his home after all. We both could see fireflies illuminating the tombstones perfectly aligned on either side of the pathway. Some of them were new while others were weathered. Some of them had dry leaves all over while others had spider webs. I could barely figure out what each one of them said.

"This is where my mother rests in peace and power!" Mohammad showed his mother's grave to me.

"I know what life without mother feels like. May God be with her soul," I said in empathy. Mysterious white mist in absolute dark gulped us entirely as we walked further into the nether-realm. We wandered there for a while and soon saw a small hut lit with few yellow dots of light.

"That's where my father spends his nights after serving the dead during the days," pointed Mohammad. After coming closer, we discovered those yellow dots were dim flames of fire emerging out of few candles and one lantern which was hung on a wooden plank inside the hut.

"Those who love soil are brought here to be buried, while those who love fire go there to be cremated," he showed me another piece of barren land besides that hut. We had to cross that cremation ground to reach that shelter. As we entered the field, we felt the warmth in the dry air due to partially burnt wood logs and hot ashes of the mortals. I was silent as my mind was full of ambivalent emotions. I felt as if scattered unburnt chunks of bones scowled at me. As the cemetery was built near the river, I listened to the clattering sound of the Ganges. As I continued to walk step by step, the lie of life freed me from its clutches, and the universal truth of death swept over breath by breath.

"Your father forgot to lock the door. See… It's partially open. Anyone can sneak in and steal his stuff," I could not resist and brought that into Mohammad's notice.

"No human physically visits here in the night. It is only their psyche and other nocturnal birds and animals who wander around this place. Moreover, who would come to steal things from this house for it has got nothing but an old man inside," he smiled and reassured me that everything was alright.

'Tuk-tuk-tuk…' as I climbed up the steps of that wooden staircase, a thumping sound emerged.

"Shh..shhh… Slow down! Father must be in deep slumber," whispered Mohammad and we both silently tread, one after another, through that ramshackle wooden door. As soon as I entered inside, I heard a soft snoring sound coming from inside one of the two small rooms in that hut. While passing by, I saw an old man lying freely on the floor and in a deep slumber. Being completely unaware of his surroundings, he slept like a baby. The perfect silence aided to his peace and no wonder he was at absolute ease. I stood outside that room for a few seconds. Seeing someone sleeping so peacefully induced a calm in my mind and body. Mohammad proceeded towards another room, and I just followed him.

"This is where you would sleep tonight," he informed me. The room was smaller than the previous one but big enough for me to lay down and be lost in the world of trance. There was an earthen pot filled with water too. What else could I ask for? I lied down on the wooden floor. Meanwhile, Mohammad blew out all the candles and dimmed the flame of the lantern and began walking towards the outside of the house. Upon asked about where he was heading to, Mohammad smiled back and told me that we both shall meet again with each other by the astounding wills of destiny.

Being exhausted by the hardships I had gone through that day, it became challenging for me to ponder upon his strange statement. All that I heard before being lapped into the world of dreams was a soft thud of the door that Mohammad closed upon exiting. The old man in the room next to me snored gutturally, and I felt a gradual decrease in that sound. Instead, I lost my consciousness to the night. Utterly clueless about what the next morning would bring to the life, I gave away myself to my pursuers, to the exhaustion and to the sleep.

10: The Shocking Revelation

EKLAVYA

'Hey! Wake up… you… hey!' I felt a few strong nudges and woke up in an instant, finding Mohammad's father waking me up with a surprised reaction resulted by my unexpected presence in that house. Rays of the morning sun passing through one of the windows embellished his face.

"Who are you? What brought you here to this deserted land?" he asked.

"I am Eklavya. I lived in a village located on the south shore of Ganga. Mohammad brought me here with him and offered a job," I replied with a shaky voice as I was a little afraid to see the expression of shock on old man's face.

"What… What job? And what did you just say! Who brought you here??"

"Mohammad, your son," I repeated.

"I don't have any son. I never had any child. What are you talking about, kid?" he asserted.

"Haha! You are good at joking; I must tell you. Mohammad never said anything about you being so humorous," I laughed it away with ease.

"Get out of my house! Leave this land right now!!" he shouted with sheer anger in his voice. I was now alarmed and in shock.

"I don't understand what is happening with me. Mohammad saved me from ending my life, he came along with me on the ferry... He showed me his mother's grave last night and cautioned me to climb up the stairs slowly so that you could sleep undisturbed... he then left, assuring me he would meet me very soon. Where is he?" I was overwhelmed and sobbed in innocence, calming the anger of the old man. Seeing me as clueless as himself, the old man asked me to have a seat and offered some water.

"I can't get my head around what you just said. All I know is that I never had any child and there is no way anyone could tell you about my wife and her grave. She died more than forty-eight years ago! No one remembers me, her or her grave! Since then I have been taking care of this place and will be taking care of this place until I die," he continued, "I never asked anyone to help me. Seeing you sleeping in my house set a panic inside me. That is why I woke you up in a fussy manner. I am sorry for that," he further explained to me. I was now alright, but my mind boggled with questions.

"So who was Mohammad? Where did he come from? Where did he go? How could he come exactly before I was about to end my life by taking a plunge into the mighty waters of the Ganges? How could he persuade me to work with him in this cemetery? How could he show your wife's grave to me last night? How could he know that you were sleeping in your room and asked me to step up slowly on the stairs? How?" I was restless.

"Show me that grave," he commanded me, wanting to test whether I lied to him or not. I stood up rapidly, and the old man followed me. Making my way through that cremation ground and passing by hundreds of graves in that cemetery I reached near the main gate. I took him exactly where Mohammad pointed out his mother's grave last night and said, "here lies your wife." There was nothing written on the weathered tombstone. The old man turned pale and numb for a few moments. That was exactly the same grave where he buried his wife about five decades ago. It became evident to him that I did not lie.

"He told me you sent him to the holy city of Banaras to study in a *Gurukul* when he was quite young. He was lost when he met me yesterday and could not find his way back home. Thus, he asked for my help and insisted that I come along with him here, to you," I further explained. The old man simply kept nodding his head sideways to deny the very existence of Mohammad, his son. Tears flowed out of his eyes.

"He was none other than the Prophet, peace be upon him! He saved your life. Kid, you must have got some bigger tasks to do in the future. Prophet Mohammad saved your life!" he said, hugging me. I was still not sure if it was the Prophet himself.

I could not fully understand what happened to me in the last one day. Series of surreal events occurred so quickly that everything seemed like a nightmare. Before I could understand or speak anything, I saw a bunch of people coming towards the cemetery. There were men, children and few women in the group. I knew someone had died and people were bringing in the dead body as there was nothing except that cemetery in the deserted land and moreover, people never came into the graveyard for recreational purposes. Having never seen a deceased person so closely before made me restless and I immediately drew the attention of the old man into that group of individuals.

The old man saw people coming closer and had a neutral expression on his face. I understood that he was habitual of seeing dead bodies daily. Soon we both realised that the deceased was primarily either of Hindu or Buddhist faith as those people headed towards cremation ground and not the graveyard. Four people carried the bier of the dead on their shoulders. The bier was ramshackle but still operational. They reached the middle of the cremation field and put that bier down on the ground. It was time for the old man to go see them. He asked me to accompany him.

"Come with me little boy, this land shall give you the strength to walk alone through the dark side of the mornings and in the loneliness of the nights." I was nervous and hesitant, but that did not limit my desire to see the truth closely. Mystic words of the wise old man propelled positive energy in my soul and thus, I followed him in the direction where people were coming from. How could I have foreseen what was going to happen that day?

11: A Sudden Demise

OLD MAN

"Where do you come from?" I questioned the group, collectively. It was a part of my daily job to know what village the dead body belonged to.

"We are from the nearby village to the south shore of the river," replied one of the four bearers.

"Whom do you bring here today?" I further asked.

"We don't know!" said another bier holder. Hearing that unexpected response from the bearer surprised me and I could see subtle signs of wondering on Eklavya's face too. I was in sheer surprise as it was for the first time that the people who brought a dead body didn't know about it.

"How come you don't know anything about the person whom you are carrying bier of? Why would you lie to me!" I asked. Eklavya listened to our conversation quietly.

"I live on the outskirts of the village to the south. We are a small community who mainly survives by selling fruits, vegetables and wood produced by the forest. While I was going to the jungle along with these fellow community members to collect some wood, I saw this man lying on the ground. At first, I thought it was some drunken who slept on the side of the road. We never saw anyone sleeping on that pathway before. There was something unusual about him weirdly lying on the ground. So, I took a closer look. I tried to wake him up only to find out he was no more," said the man in a painful voice.

"There was no way we could identify him. Also, it was too late for the body to be kept in the condition in which it was lying on the road. So we brought him here. That is what we all could think of at that time," said another person from the group. Their story seemed to be genuine, and I was convinced now. Though an unclaimed body had never arrived in the past that never meant that it can't happen ever. The world needed more of such good people in the age of *Kali,* people who sometimes don't let things go as they may, taking responsibility and control of the situation.

"You must buy wood logs and a linen shroud from me for cremating this dead body," said I and with my words, a commotion began in the group. People looked at each other and murmured something. They told each other their own superficial reasons for not having money. Seemed like nobody wanted to pay for the wood and shroud for that deceased person. I was old and with age became wise enough to judge their behaviour and knew people wouldn't spend their hard-earned money on someone who is dead and that too not among their known. Despite being so sure about those people not willing to pay me, I insisted as that was the only source of my income. Those who used cremation ground and graveyard bought wood, shroud, incense sticks and other required stuff from me. People had to buy these items for disposal of the dead bodies. However, this time nobody cared about the proper and rightful disposal of the corpse as it was unclaimed, nobody knew the deceased. In fact, they all indeed expected some acknowledgement and praises for themselves for their good deed, for they brought in the dead body to the cremation ground.

"Neither I can give you the wood and shroud required to dispose of this body in this cremation ground without receiving the money, nor I can let you put this dead body here. Take it back right now!" I had to be adamant. Eklavya listened and perhaps pondered upon the situation, and then he spoke,

"Please let them cremate this body for free. I shall work for you without expecting any monetary benefit from this job, in return of your generosity towards these people and the deceased," he said with a suggestive tone.

"You don't have to do that. Why would you do such a thing for someone you don't even know?" I asked surprisingly.

"No matter come what may, mankind must not let humanity die, ever, for it is humanity that defines humankind and not contrariwise! To me, he is a human, and that is enough to know about him," he responded confidently. His firm and thoughtful voice left all of us stunned. Seeing a young teenager having such powerful thoughts made all those people realise their worth which indeed, seemed too little. They were ashamed of their inhumane psychology but couldn't do much about it. Without waiting for any affirmative approval from my side, Eklavya stepped ahead and decided to take a look at the dead body.

He stood idly near the body for a few seconds and then fell to the ground unconsciously. Everybody thought it was because he never saw any deceased person before. I rushed to bring some water to sprinkle on his sweating face. As soon as he woke up, he lost his conscious again. Now everyone became concerned about him. I tried pouring some more water onto his face. He quickly rose up and kept on sitting on the ground. His eyes turned red, full of tears and he shook his head vigorously.

"You must go inside now, I will take care of this body," I was worried about him and commanded. He looked at me with a shattered gaze, tears pouring down his eyes.

"He is my father! He was my father! Oh! Lord, what have you done? Why!! Father... wake up, wake up please!!" Eklavya lost his voice momentarily due to the extreme emotional outburst. Everyone standing there had their eyes filled with tears. I went in sheer shock. Never in my lifetime before, I had been so nervous as I was at that time. I held Eklavya, raised him and made him stand on the ground. I too cried seeing him in tears.

"Don't cry, my child! Death is inevitable, if this is what He (God) wants, be it so, don't cry dear," my words fell short, but I somehow tried to pacify Eklavya while crying out of agony.

"Why him? Why now?? Is that what Mohammad brought me here for?!" he tightly held the dead body of his father, Vyas. Vyas was not recognisable as his clothes were mostly worn out, he had long, ungroomed beard, his body stank as filth from the gutter.

"He once was the most respected man in the village. People deemed him as a saint, and he was called *Purushottam* for his good deeds to others," Eklavya told everybody collectively.

Seeing that dramatic tragedy of a child, the very same people who earlier disowned that dead body and didn't wish to pay any money for the shroud and wood collected money for Vyas's cremation. Eklavya had no words for those people. He had to understand that there was nothing he could do to bring his father back. To him, death was not the end of the life. Instead, it was the beginning of new life in a different realm. I did not take anything from those people and provided them with all the required materials for free. Eklavya performed the last rites under my supervision. He cried vigorously, taking one more blame on his fate for letting his father die. It was too much for an innocent child to take on to. He recalled how so-called his people in the village deemed him as a sullied child. He remembered that day when he decided to leave his village permanently, rather he was forced to leave his home forever. Those accusations of killing his mother right after his birth... Those deaths caused by the flood in the

Ganges even before he was born, the painful and miserable death of *Amma*, Vyas losing his sanity in vain and now the tragic demise of his father... killed Eklavya's will to seek God and the universal truth behind all of the worldly aspirations. *Kali*, the evil targeted innocent and pure souls like Eklavya as all others were already under the demonic influence of *Kali Yuga*. One who possessed a strong will to seek God and know the truth became weak with each passing day.

"How could God, who is said to be perfect, can create something so imperfect, something full of flaws?" Eklavya screamed.

He saw many deaths, so much of hardships that his belief in God diminished with each passing day. His rainy days made him stronger, emotionally or maybe he became emotionless. The holy fire enfolded the dead body of Vyas entirely into its might. Eventually, people gathered around the burning pyre retreated towards their homes, workplaces and to wherever they had to go. Eklavya with his watery eyes along with me waited until flames of fire subsided.

"We have to collect the mortal remains of your father tomorrow morning," I said.

"Yes, I know I have to offer them to the holy Ganga," he looked up at the sky, raised his finger and claimed in shattered voice... "On the day of judgement, I will let God have a chance to explain everything he did to me!" We both headed towards the hut.

12: The Passage of Time

TIME

The next morning, Eklavya left the hut for traditional disposal of his father's mortal remains in the Ganges. The river was nearby, so he reached it in no time. He walked into the river and felt a cold shivering sensation in his body. Eklavya kept on going until water level reached his chest. A strong wind splashed river water on his face, and he got that freezing water inside his ears too. And then all he could hear was his heart pounding. He poured that mixture of ashes and bone chunks in the water of the Ganges, with his hands folded and hoping for a peaceful abode of his father's soul on its way back to the heavens. After coming back to the cemetery, he went straight into the cottage. The old man kept himself busy in outside works. He saw Eklavya going inside the hut but did not say anything as he knew that Eklavya would take some time to recover from this tragedy.

A year passed witnessing Eklavya bearing the weight of silence for most of the time during the days and releasing that burden of silence by sobbing weakly during the nights. He never realised that the old man was acutely aware of his acts of shedding tears in the memory of his loved ones. Eklavya's situation often reminded the old man about his wife and the good early days spent with her.

That, in turn, enticed an emotional outburst in his heart, making him cry with a muzzled mouth.

Eklavya's scars began healing with the flow of time. He became less and less upset with the past and assisted the old man in managing the cemetery. Seeing and helping people performing the last rites of the dead bodies of their loved ones became less and less terrifying for him. He understood the cycle of life. To him, death was not something to fear about anymore. Though it wasn't possible for him to completely detach himself from the tragic past yet he knew that he could not change that. Whatever happened, happened and he must live with that without letting his present and future affected by it.

Time and tide wait for none. It seemed like a few more years had passed in a split of a second, just like that! The old man became even older, incapable of doing any physical work. Eklavya learned a lot by that time, and he did almost everything the old man did before. There were times when he required some guidance from the old man. Eklavya entered his teenage. As his body was undergoing lots of physical changes, his mind evolved too. He became even wise and more mature than he was before. He would go to the jungle and cut the trees. He would then chop the trunk into small wood logs suitable for cremation of the dead bodies. For each tree gone down because of his actions, Eklavya planted two trees in the jungle. He prepared several death beds from that wood, ensuring timely cremation of the dead bodies. He also maintained another field in which people used to bury the dead.

Eklavya and the old man happily accepted whatever people gave them in exchange for their service. Soon people recognised his efforts as he was well settled in the society. He often trained children in martial arts in the fields nearby. It gave him a chance to hone his skills learned in the *Gurukul* on the one hand and kept him from recalling his tragic past on the other. Eklavya also made tools and weapons from whatever he could get from his hut and the jungle.

His involvement in the pain of the people made him an integral part of the community. People appreciated his dedication to work and behaviour with other people. Eklavya was satisfied with his work. It seemed that he gave up on worldly desires. He believed in God, but he was very far away from falling into the clutches of the religions on earth. He neither praised any religion, nor he maligned any. He realised that death does not discriminate between religions, castes, colours, creeds and races. Death, according to him represented an incredible example of serving everyone with equality.

Like his father, Eklavya also wanted to devote his life for the betterment of the society and its people. He acknowledged his past, but he always refused to believe in the reasons given to him for his tragic past. He was just not ready to accept that it was him behind the demise of his loved ones, he never deemed himself cursed anymore. Instead, he was determined to search for the reasons behind everything happened to him.

Moreover, he wanted to know why people in his village began acting and behaving like strangers all of a sudden. He had to remove that burden of being 'sullied' from his soul. Thus, he planned to visit *Maha-Purohit* in his village again to see what was going on there. He never wanted to leave the old man all by himself and strangled with the burden of cemetery work. All he waited for, was the right time to take a short leave from his job.

13: An Uninvited Guest

EKLAVYA

It was a beautiful morning of the summer season as the sun had just risen. Wind blowing towards the shore swept off the waters of the Ganges and transformed itself into the cool soothing breeze and served as a panacea to the heat of summer sun. The voices of local sailors in the Ganges could also be heard. They shouted out loud at potential customers to attract them to their respective boats. Flocks of birds chirped vigorously as if they prepared to form a legion against their predators. The thumping sound of wet clothes being smashed against the shore-side rocks echoed simultaneously. Washermen had to do their job every morning. This thumping of clothes on the stone made a patterned sound effect. The rustling sound of the wind, as it blew through trees, proved itself to be the most admired form of the symphony that gently woke me up.

With my one eye opened, I ran a quick check of the surroundings. I knew that the old man got up before me as usual.

'How does he sleep so late and wake up so early every day?' I wondered while lying on the floor and soon after, heard a thud and then 'ruff...ruff...shing, ruff...ruff...shing' kind of sound coming from the field. Seemed like someone was shovelling off the soil and digging in the land. I took a look outside the window and knew what was happening. Seeing the old man digging in the earth did not make any sense to me at first. And so, I collected my clothes as I was going to the river bank to take a bath in the Ganges. The icy cold water of the river always made bathing fun in the summers. A lot of people enjoyed taking the plunge into the river. I came outside the hut with all my grooming and bathing stuff along with some clothes, only to see that the old man had dug a grave in the land, right beside where he buried his wife almost five decades ago. Surprised by his action, I deliberately rushed outside.

"Why would you do that? I see no dead body here!" I asked him.

"This one is for me, child," he replied and further added, "My life is withering away with each passing day. I wish to rest in peace right here, next to my beloved wife in this grave."

"Alright! But why would you dig your own grave in advance? This seems weird," I wanted to know the reason behind him digging his grave.

"Buying space here in this barren land is becoming more and more expensive. Better safe than sorry, I reserved my spot! Haha!" he tried to deviate my mind, joking with me but failed miserably.

"Your actions are out of my understanding. You are really getting old now!" I murmured while nodding my head sideways and headed towards the shore. He smiled and went inside the hut.

OLD MAN

"Tuk…tuk…tuck" someone tapped on the door. It had not been much longer since Eklavya left. 'There is no way he (Eklavya) could return this quick from the shore,' I wondered while walking towards the door to see who was on the other side. 'Eeeerrrrkkk' that ramshackle door opened,

"I am sorry I don't have any money to give you today. I might be able to help you in the evening if I make any earnings today," I said and shut the door instantly.

"Tuk.Tuk.Tuk..tuck" the person on the door knocked vigorously again. I got annoyed with that tapping of the door; less because someone unknown stood at the door, more because I feared that one sturdy knock would completely damage that already weak door.

"What is that you want from me?", frustration was apparent inside my mind and perhaps on my face too.

"I am not here to ask for money, gentleman. I am here to take back something of much more importance," said the person at the door.

"I am unable to get you. What is that I can give you?" I further asked.

"Where is Eklavya?" he interrogated.

"There is no one in the house. I don't know what you are talking about. You are wasting my time, go away! Come again, never!" I almost yelled at him and shut the door in anger.

'How come he knows that Eklavya is here? Who is he? Thank God, Eklavya is not here now,' I had my mind full of questions and worries. By that time, Eklavya would have recollected his stuff and walked back home.

"You were laughing when I left, what happened that you seem so concerned now?" Eklavya upon reaching home asked after seeing me in distress.

"There was a knock on the door soon after you left. Someone asked about you. He was here to take you back with him. I don't know who he was, I never saw him around before. But I am worried how does he know about you being here. Moreover, why would a eunuch want to take you with him? Do you know him?" I finished asking and eagerly waited for his answer.

"No way! I don't know anyone here except you," he instantly assured me.

"Alright! Since you don't know anyone except…"

"Wait a minute! Did you just say, eunuch?? Was he tall and had a small bag hung on his neck? Had he applied makeup on his face?" Eklavya interrupted and bombarded a series of questions one after another.

"Well, almost every eunuch here has this general appearance," I answered.

"Did he bear a coloured mark of *trishula* on his forehead??" Eklavya remembered and asked me to confirm what he guessed for that eunuch.

"Yes! He had a *trishula* on his forehead," I recalled and told him.

"*Maha-Purohit*! He was *Maha-Purohit* from my village. Why would he come here, how did he know about me being here? Which direction did he go to..." he rushed outside and slammed shut the door.

'Dear Lord! I don't want to spend my hard earned money on this door again,' I tilted my head upwards and thought in my mind. Subconsciously, I was shocked to know that *Maha-Purohit* was a eunuch.

"A newly born baby was hated by everyone in the village without doing anything to deserve that hate. My only fault was not being born up the way it was expected of me."

-    Maha-Purohit *(Long Live the Sullied)*

14: The Culprit Priest

EKLAVYA

A few days ago, I thought of going back to my village and seek *Maha-Purohit* for I was curious to know what had happened and how did that happen. However, by the astounding wills of the fate, *Maha-Purohit* himself walked to me. How could I have let go of that opportunity so big then? 'The one who is pretty accurate in telling the future must explain the past to me.' I had this thought running through my mind continuously. Restlessly and aimlessly, with a hope that I would find all the answers to my questions, I moved here and there on each path and in every direction possible, shouting out '*Maha-Purohit! Maha-Purohit!*' loud but could not locate him. With my heart heavy, hopelessly and atrociously with my head held down, I sat under a tree in despair.

Tremors of sorrow clutched my heart, and I felt being lynched by the destiny once again. With my eyes wet, I looked straight ahead and noticed a person coming towards me. He appeared to be a farmer by his outlook and was happily humming a melody. Not wanting that stranger to know of my cry, I swept my tears quickly. He did not notice me sitting under the tree and kept on walking. And as he passed by the tree which I was sitting under, I heard what he thrummed.

'Oh, Voyager! Why do you stress over sorrow?... distress is our companion! Happiness is, however, a fleeting shadow, as it goes back and forth... but sorrow is our friend, it remains with us! If the destination is far and life seems harsh on you, so be it... Is God's affection any less intense? Regardless of the possibility that there is an enormous number of thistles in a way, is His (God's) love any less intense? Oh, traveller, do you have faith in Him? Amid the sorrow just light up lights of the path in your eyes... In such a big world in long desolate ways, Oh! Traveller, do you have faith in Him!?' The farmer continued to go away, and so did his voice until it vanished completely. But I listened to his song, and it got me a new zeal inside my heart. I thought as if he was meant to cross the path at the same time when I sat there. He appeared to be ignoring my presence on purpose, and his appearance too was like that of Mohammad.

I woke up from my partial unconsciousness and walked towards the direction where that stranger had gone. 'So what if *Maha-Purohit* went away... I can go by myself to visit him,' I thought in hope and kept walking. I didn't find the stranger on the way. Soon, I realised that I was on the path which would take me to the cemetery and to my home.

Upon reaching home, I found *Maha-Purohit* and the old man sitting together, engaged in some serious conversation.

"Here you come! Soon after you left, *Maha-Purohit* knocked on the door again. Since you already told me about who he was, I let him in," the old man explained to me even before I asked about how come *Maha-Purohit* was inside the house. I greeted *Maha-Purohit* and said, "I planned to visit you in my village."

"I too came here to discuss something important with you," he replied.

"How do you know that I live here?" I asked.

"Your friend Mahavir told me about you." After listening to this, I shockingly looked at *Maha-Purohit* for a moment.

"Who Mahavir?!!" I questioned, apparently to both Maha-Purohit and the old man. They both looked utterly clueless as I expected of them.

"He told his name was Mahavir and that he is your friend. You both first met on the bank of river Ganga. Remember?" *Maha-Purohit* tried to remind me about Mahavir, a person whom I had never met in my life. The old man and I knew that he was none other than Mohammad. However, we were unable to get our head around as to why Mohammad changed his name to Mahavir. After being asked about why we both were so surprised and confused, I let *Maha-Purohit* know everything from the beginning, telling him about how Mohammad and I met and under what circumstances and what all had happened that day. He was equally surprised after listening about Mohammad.

"Both Mahavir and Mohammad were prophets," he said after thinking for some time.

"Prophets are contributing their bit to put everything right on track for the final showdown between you and the *Kali*. Your life is not just an ordinary life. It must have a bigger purpose. It shall create history, Eklavya!" He further added.

"Eklavya, I will tell you the reason why I came here to take you back to the village. I have to confess some things to you," he further continued, and the old man and I went all ears.

"Vyas was venerated as a saint in the village. His wise and honest deeds were always appreciated by all the villagers. This created fear in my mind, making me insecure about my position and power. I worried that one day, people will treat Vyas equally and gradually even more respectfully than they treated me. I lived in constant fear that one day my hard work and legacy will be ruined by your father's good deeds. The evil of *Kali Yuga* had me trapped in its grip." *Maha-Purohit*'s voice shook and went a few levels down, his eyes were wet. The old man and I looked at him with our eyes wide open.

"It all started about twenty-one years ago when your father, Vyas and some elders invited me to bless your mother, Sumati and to predict the nature, time and day of your birth. It took me so long to calculate and understand what impact would stars and planets put on your birth. I realised that the day and nature of your birth was one of the rarest and most auspicious events in astrology. But I did not want you to come into this world... I did not want you to be born! The entire village looked forward to seeing the scion of Ikshvaku. Whereas, I planned on how to malign the legacy of Vyas and to kill you even before your birth. I met your father on the way when he left for the neighbouring village to buy some seeds for agriculture. I knew your mother would give birth to you later that night. I could have easily reminded Vyas and stopped him from going far away from Sumati. But I did not! I could not!! I saw that as an opportunity to kill you, as you and your mother were weak and vulnerable. When the storm occurred in the Ganges, I expected it would kill your father. Several died in the river while commuting, many died on land, but Vyas survived. I had already planted the seeds of your destruction when I visited your family to predict your birth. The medicinal herbs that I gave to your mother to supplement her with necessary nutrition during pregnancy were meant to kill you! But with God's will, she gave birth to you and sacrificed her life. I had no intention to harm Sumati. Now I understand that you were destined to be born, Eklavya...

After your departure to the *Gurukul*, *Amma* remained depressed. She once saw me grabbing herbs from the *Vaidya* and throwing it in the garbage. My action of forcefully handing him over another herb and her continuously deteriorating condition after taking those herbs had given *Amma* strong hints of what I did against her. She was wise enough to figure that conspiracy out. She was a threat to me, a danger to my subtle and respected image!! She was in her last days and often created chaos for me. There were times when she tried to convince Vyas about my intentions and cruel actions against her and Vyas. Vyas, however, neglected her as he never thought that I as *Maha-Purohit* could do such demeaning, inhumane deeds. It was then when I decided to put *Amma* on eternal sleep by giving her poison. That would clear one more obstacle from my path, and I thought that distress would definitely shatter and break Vyas forever.

My actions produced results. Vyas became quieter and isolated with each passing day. But he was still kind and useful to others occasionally. His belief in God was unshakable, and that is why he always remained sane. Seeing myself failing big time, I decided to do something else.

While you were in the *Gurukul*, away from your village, I persuaded people about how misfortunate your family and the entire community became after your birth. That seemed to be working! As I jinxed them day by day, they accepted the fake reality of you and your father being unholy. They were all determined to reject you both as Ikshvakus. I cultivated a 'sullied' image of yours in their minds. Poor, they! They trusted and showed so much confidence in whatever I told them about you. Your people were too innocent to know what was going on. People kept themselves from talking, seeing or meeting with Vyas. They would not acknowledge his presence at all. This abandonment slowly killed Vyas from inside. He did not have any idea of what happened to the people in that village. As a result of that weird treatment and conditioning, Sumati's death, *Amma*'s death and your absence, Vyas was left alone and lonely. He was all by himself in that village full of people, yet deserted for him, and thus, he lost his sanity. Nobody took any care of him. His lands were taken by the villagers, and he was banished from entering his own neighbourhood and house. Vyas had to beg for food and clothes. Three years of torture was more than enough to make your father mentally ill.

And then you came back from the *Gurukul* only to discover that you were discarded by your own people. You found out that you were deemed as a 'sullied' and unholy child in the village. Luckily, you saw me that day, and I added fuel to the fire by testifying that you were 'cursed' indeed. Then I compelled you to leave your people, your own village. My agenda was accomplished that day, and when I saw you crying after seeing Vyas in devastating condition, I was so relieved! For decades, I worshipped God and gained nothing but false hopes that one day I will be acknowledged as the most celebrated priest and astrologer of all times. I wanted to become an influencer in the society. And for the first time, I admired evil and look, what it did to you and your family!

The order is just a dream of man; Chaos, the law of nature. How could my life be at peace after doing such monstrous acts and with those who have pure and pious souls!... Few days after *Amma*'s death and after Vyas had entirely gone out of the control of his faculties, the

Sarpanch found a pile of the secret document from *Amma*'s house. It has been rightly said that what goes around, comes all the way back around. Karma and kismet played their roles perfectly in *Kali Yuga*. That document was a record of few pieces of writings *Amma* wrote. Since no one believed *Amma* in her last days, as everyone thought of her as someone who had lost all her sanity and consciousness, she wrote everything on paper. With a hope that one day someone would find that hidden pile and expose my reality, she wrote whatever she deemed to be correct about my actions. *Sarpanch* revealed that document in *panchayat* that brought my truth in front of everyone. Everything made sense! She wrote about me manipulating people against Vyas. She wrote that she found something was wrong with Sumati in her pregnancy days. Also, she insisted that Sumati's death was not natural. It was my herbs which caused her death.

Amma with her experience could determine that the medicines which I gave to your mother were something else. She could also predict my intentions to kill her and specifically wrote '*Maha-Purohit* is not what he seems to be. *Kali* has taken over him, and he has turned into a monster! I saw him throwing away my medicinal herbs and forcefully handing something else to the *Vaidya* to give me. That 'something' is putting me to eternal sleep. He knows I saw him doing it and now, he fears me and might try to kill me as he did to Sumati.'

I was then called to the *panchayat*. The *Vaidya* accepted that he was forcefully handed over some unknown wild herbs by me to be given to *Amma*. He confessed that he could not resist me as I held a senior authority over him as *Maha-Purohit* of the region and he had no clear idea that those herbs were poisonous. Everybody looked at me with disgust, and I felt their rage for me. I pleaded guilty as I did not want to live with the burden of such demonic deeds on my soul... I was ready to accept whatever punishment would the council decide for me, even if it was a death penalty! But they all declared me 'sullied' and threw me out of the village as I did to you.

Trust me... Death seemed to be an easy way out than being disregarded and humiliated like this!! I don't know if I can be forgiven for my sins. I am filled with remorse and shame... I am your culprit, Eklavya! Please forgive me... I am sorry!" *Maha-Purohit* cried vehemently. He leant on his knees, with his hands folded and head bent down, trying to convince me that he was in pain and deeply regretted his actions. I, on the contrary, stood still, lost in a different world and trying to believe what I just heard. Tears rolled down my eyes, and I walked out of the room. The old man appeared to be in grave trauma after listening to *Maha-Purohit*. His mind must have filled with lethal anger for *Maha-Purohit* and heart with pity emotions for my disheartening fate.

With teary eyes and his hands folded in guilt, *Maha-Purohit* walked out of the room. "Please forgive me, Son! I must be punished for this horrific character of mine...Eklavya, please forgive this sinner, I am broken from inside!" he expressed his repent. I, with each uttered word of *Maha-Purohit*, got my temperament high. But I was the son of Vyas, the *Purushottam*. How could I have lost control of my faculties so quickly? Whatever I said that day was not said by me, instead, it was my father's spirit that possibly took over my mind. I would have killed that eunuch right there right then, but something from within kept me from doing that. "Light only gets in when something's broken! Now that you are broken from inside, I shall let the light of wisdom pass through you!" I said while pointing at *Maha-Purohit*. My eyes emitted sheer anger, yet it must have given subtle hints of forgiveness for him. The old man looked at me agape. I held the arm of *Maha-Purohit* and dragged him towards the graves in the cemetery. He did not say anything and kept walking, and the old man followed both of us.

"Since ages, you have been living in oblivion, *Maha-Purohit*! You lived in this false hope that if you put my father down in the eyes of others, you will earn more respect and gain influence on the people. You were jealous of my father! You were afraid of his vital importance in the society... This seed of hatred and fear eventually grew so big that it turned your self-esteem into ego, your wisdom into absolute stupidity. You could have just chosen to do more good to others, to genuinely become greater, wiser, kinder than what my father was. But the evil took over your character, and you downgraded my father, maligning his integrity to upgrade yourself in the eyes of the people. You became the evil itself!! Your so-called high degree of intellect never reminded you that pulling others down had never been and will never be the wise and right way of progressing! Those people who got you as their *Maha-Purohit*, those villagers who trusted you and respected you with their whole heart must have been staunch sinners in the past! Weak they...as they could not even think of your actions in their dreams and were ruthlessly betrayed by you. Father always focused on what he could give rather than what he could take from others. The glory of the Father is so much so that even after his death, he has an influence on you and on the people of his village. His legacy shall keep itself alive for ages to come. Many remember him for love, many more will remember him with respect, some in vain while few in hatred. But Vyas is the name nobody will ever be able to forget for their entire lives!

Look at these graves... look around you, those burning dead bodies... we all will come here one day as death is the only truth of life. Why are you so concerned about your worldly reputation then? What did you bring with you into this world? What will you take from this world? Your false sense of happiness led to the biggest sorrows of your life. It's clear now that you pretend to observe the principles of religion only for the sake of your stature. You, *Maha-Purohit*, are just a devotee of your belly! Your appetite for vengeance has ruined your life, it has killed your character. I don't know if I would ever forgive you for your animalism. All I can suggest you is to sacrifice your remaining days for the good of the innocent. You must redeem yourself from the clutches of the evil. Stop predicting the future of others and start improving your present! I will never be able to forget what you did to my family. But you can at least do something to compensate for your sins and then upon reaching the transcendental world, ask God to forgive you. He might have some faith and hope left in you, I don't! Now before I lose myself to my pursuers, anger and rage, I insist you leave! Go away before it's too late!" I finished talking and turned my back on *Maha-Purohit*. I didn't want to see that eunuch and lose my control.

"I don't want to die for no purpose... I will not die in vain," he blabbered as if he made a solemn promise to himself and swiftly walked away from the cemetery with his head held down in shame.

"I want to go away from this cemetery," I said. "It's already late evening. Make sure you come back before it's too dark for the night," the old man suggested.

"You did not understand what I said, I seek your permission to leave you and this cemetery forever," I authoritatively made myself clear.

"Now that you have already decided to leave, who am I to question your decision?" he replied after a small pause and continued, "Do come back in time though. I fear it would be too late when you come back."

"You are not going to die anytime soon. I shall visit you soon. Please bless me!" I folded my hands and sought blessings from him. We both went into the hut, and after collecting my clothes and some books, I left the cemetery.

OLD MAN

With a heavy heart and shallow breath, I kept looking at Eklavya until he vanished in the dark.

'Eerrrr…chhrrrrr…err' two simultaneously creaking sounds of rusty gates of the cemetery was all I could hear that night after he left. I blew the lamp off and lied down on the floor.

'May there be some light of hope soon despite all this darkness!' I wished and got lost in a deep slumber.

"I had sleepless nights almost every single day, dreaming about Sumati laying dead in front of me, *Amma* telling my secrets in the *panchayat*, Eklavya killing me brutally after knowing what I did to his mother, grandmother and father. I hallucinated during the days, in between my talks and walks, seeing myself hung with the tree at the *choupal.*"

-   Maha-Purohit *(Long Live the Sullied)*

15: The Quest Begins

TIME

Half a decade ago, a sixteen-year-old left his village in search of the truth of life. He moved far away from the hypocrite world and devoted his life to seeking God. Amidst his journey, he met a mysterious man named Mohammad who made him realise that solitude was not the solution to find true-self. The boy spent five years in the cemetery working with an old man and intimately experienced the phenomenon of death only to understand the importance of human life, karma and kismet.

Eklavya was again on his journey to seek the truth. This time, not by detaching himself from the world but remaining in the world and sharing the light of wisdom with whoever he would meet in his life. This time, he was bound for another journey, away from the Himalayas and Ganga and in the hope of reaching a higher stage of civilisation.

EKLAVYA

The night prevailed over the evening. I had mostly walked away from the cemetery and had not seen anybody on my way since past few hours. Thus, I that night, had a hunch that I would not reach any place populated with human beings. I knew nothing about where that path took me. Nonetheless, that road soon ended right where the dense jungle enchanted me with its enormous span. I stopped and stood there for a few seconds, debating whether I should enter inside the heart of the forest or take my steps back onto the path that brought me there. After struggling with some thoughts and being at loggerheads with my reasoning going on inside my forlorn brain, I decided to go further into the jungle. I was hungry too and thought of eating whatever I found on my way into the forest.

The jungle appeared to be a massive fortress with giant walls of trees covered in leaves. Everything seemed to be black due to the darkness, but I could smell the woody and grassy incense which was moist enough to let me know the lush wealth that jungle had treasured in its pulse. The night sky greeted the world with twinkling stars like glinting silver aquamarines. The further I proceeded, the more awestruck and magical it became. There was no sign of animals and birds. Probably, they all were sleeping to get themselves ready for the game of 'prey or predator' the next day. However, grasshoppers and insects produced a sharp hissing sound that penetrated the silence of the night.

I felt the crisp of fallen branches underneath my steps. A little ahead lay a mattress of leaves and branches as if the wind had piled it up for me to sleep upon. I found some windfall fruits too. Most of them were unrecognisable by taste. Luckily, I found few apples that were enough to fill my stomach aptly. After feasting on those apples, I put a sheet over the leafy mattress to lay down on it. My bag containing books and clothes became a perfect pillow for the night. There was a fear inside my mind of getting pricked by the insects, being attacked by the animals and most likely, being uncertain about the upcoming day. However, the golden moon hung in the distance pacified me gently, and I gave away myself to the world of dreams.

Few droplets, cold as ice fell on my face and I opened my eyes slowly while sweeping off the water from the forehead. The first thing I saw was alpine trees standing straight in calmness and awash with a subtle glow. It took few seconds to sync into my mind that I was not at the cemetery anymore but out in the wilderness. Right after gaining control of my senses, I felt a sprain-like pain in the back as my bed was dilapidated and the bed sheet was damp for all night long. A strong quiver took over my body instantly, and I shivered uncontrollably. I immediately missed the smooth wooden floor of that ramshackle hut in the cemetery.

'What would he be doing now?' I wondered in my mind about the old man, stood up, folding my sheet and putting it in the bag. The jungle had completely become a different place than what it was in the night. Grasshoppers and insects were silent, and birds created a symphony of songs. It seemed to be an ancient jungle, growing seamlessly and proudly in every direction possible. Huge trees and little plants stood silently and looked like sentinels of the orchard watchfully guarding its glory. I walked ahead in search of water and food. As I went further into the jungle, I almost lost the idea of the directions. However, the position of the Sun gave me a slight hint of what direction I was heading to. 'There must be many sources of water in this jungle. All I have to do is find one for myself!' I set a small goal and motivated myself. 'Ahh!! Oh! Lord...' my foot got scratched by a pointy pine leaf as I stepped onto it unknowingly. It was then when my survival instincts kicked in. So far, I was so awestruck by the beauty of the jungle that I never realised it could pose a threat to my life. I followed a small herd of deer from a safe distance, in the hope that those would lead me to where water was. A few minutes later I felt the wet earth underneath and my heart filled with joy after discovering a freshwater pond. Without further due, I ran towards it, drank plenty of water as I was thirsty from last night and washed my face. The pool was so fresh and with a hint of mint that it made me forget everything for a moment.

After revitalising my body and mind with a quick bath, I sat under a tree and ate some more fruits I had collected last night. The wind whistled around the trunk of the tree, disturbing the leaves and produced a rustling sound. I could smell a smoky fragrance mixed with decaying wood aroma and saw some wild lizards scrabbling on tree barks. I was continuously pondering what I would do next. I was left with some options, either I could continue my journey and hope that it would take me somewhere safe, or I could go back to the cemetery, or I could wait there for an undetermined duration and wish that someone would rescue me out of the jungle. Several random thoughts wrestled with each other in my mind. Finally, I chose to keep on walking further and see what destiny had to offer. Making my way through detritus in the path, puzzling directions, ginormous swamps and protecting myself from dangerous animals, wild fruits and berries I walked for several hours at a stretch.

Several hours of continuous walk and still stranded in the middle of nowhere! I was tired and a little disappointed too. At times, I regretted my decision of leaving the cemetery. With fear in my mind of surviving one more night in the jungle, I sat down to catch some breath. There were times during my journey when I felt like surrendering my future to uncertainty, I felt like giving up on the purpose of my life. But my willpower knew no equal, and I stood rock solid on my determinations. I walked again, this time with double the pace and even with stronger zeal. I tackled knobby roots, rough surfaces, humid air, churring insects, skunks, dead animals, fear of wild animals, rotting smell and what not! My hard work and optimism finally produced results, when I saw a small but firmly standing cabin at a distance. It was mostly made up of clay and hay. I thought twice before knocking on the door of that shed as I feared that I would not be welcomed into the cabin or what if there is nobody but wild creatures inside it. But I knew I would not know what was going to happen unless I take my chances.

In God's name, I went near the cabin and knocked on the door with hesitation. The wooden door was in a devastating condition. Moulds and mushrooms grew on its decaying wood. 'This door is way too ugly than what old man has in his hut', I thought. As soon as I knocked on the door, it opened by itself, making a 'chhhrrr' kind of sound. It was evident to me that nobody was there in the shed. I was relieved and confused at the same time. Relieved, for I had nobody to encounter and confused, for I might have to deal with something or someone more intense and dangerous afterwards. As the night slowly gulped the Sun, I decided to stay and spend the night in the cabin. The cabin happened to be abandoned. It had an old lamp without any fuel in it, an earthen pot filled with dirty, muddy water, and a shelf on which some booklets were lying since ages. I grabbed one out of interest and discovered those were spiritual and meditation booklets. Even more, that cabin was shared by spiders in huge spider-webs, lizards on the floor, scattered remains of nests made by the birds, few shrubberies trying to make their way through the clay floor, dead and alive insects and few rodents that quickly hid right after my entry.

I was exhausted, and I would have done anything and everything in desperation just to get some sleep. How could I not accept that cabin then? Despite being so exposed and vulnerable to those weird creatures, I was happy, for being inside that cabin was still better and safer than being out in the wild. With a hope that nothing serious will happen and that I would not be harmed by those creatures I shut the door and squeezed myself into a corner, keeping an eye on those lizards that were eating insects. I could barely see them due to the darkness. However, maintaining an eye on them would ensure that I am safe from those lizards. There were times when I could not locate them at all, and then it scared the hell out of me.

After a while, I somehow braved those creatures. I recalled my past few days and all that happened to me. And then I wanted to see the serene glimpse of the night sky as I saw it last night before sleeping. Suddenly, I heard a loud roar of the clouds, furiously bright flashes of lights began haunting the jungle, and it started pouring seconds after that. A smile appeared on my face as nature had just toyed with my desire to see the night sky. But I was thankful to the universe for protecting me from that rain.

Figure: Shattered cabin in the jungle.

16: The Abduction

EKLAVYA

"How have you been these days, Son?... I eagerly waited for an endless duration of time just to see you once!" I heard an echoing voice coming from some direction.

"Look at you! You have become like your father. Come to me, my child... I want to spend some time with my lovely Son!" Upon coming closer to the voice, I saw a lady dressed in bright white fabric calling my name and stretching her arms to get hold of me.

"Mother! Is that you??... Maa...?" I asked anxiously. She smiled and nodded her head in affirmative. "Where have you been Maa? Where were you when I needed you the most?? You know, they threw me out of my home and killed Father and *Amma*!!" I sobbed.

"I want to come with you... I don't like this world anymore!!" I further added.

"You are meant to change the course of time, Son. My child would not lose his hope. I am with you always... I have been with you for the last twenty-one years now," she said and began walking away from where I was standing.

"Maa! Maa!! Please come back, Maa...!" I woke up in a snap and sat down, discovering that I literally screamed after waking up from that dream. Tears fell from my eyes, my body profusely sweated, I was out of breath and in shock too. I realised it was just a dream, a weirdly intense dream. For the first time in my life, I saw my mother, though I didn't see her face.

The night was half past, and it was still pouring heavily. The cabin developed some leaks on its ceiling. I felt a cold sensation in my entire body and tried putting myself back to sleep again but just could not. That dream left me in the state of incredulity, making me wonder what it meant. I debated as to why would I dream of my mother after so many years of her death and thought about what she was trying to say to me. 'How would I change the course of time... Why did Maa say that?' This question continuously kept setting a panic in my mind.

After wondering about what had happened, I gradually emerged out of the shock from my dream. I recovered soon and was about to sleep again but heard a strange voice from very far away. 'Hoo...Ham...Ho!...Ho!' The sound slowly came closer. It seemed as if a large group of people were on some mission. Their language was also different.

Spooky night, torrential rains, that strange dream and then those people screaming something unearthly were enough to scare me to the core of my heart. Seemed like the universe tested my limits. 'Swisshh...Swish..' two consecutive sounds occurred, and their screaming stopped too. They killed some animal apparently. There was absolute silence in the area except for the sound that rain made. Now, that silence created a horrific state in my mind, so much so that I began expecting a deadly attack on myself. 'Now someone among them will suddenly come and kill me... Who are they?... What do they look like... How will they kill me, will they enter from the door or they would break these clay walls?? What can I do now... I should have gone back to the cemetery... I am not afraid of death, all death is certain, but I don't want to be killed like this! Oh, Lord! Is this the end of me??' in seconds, my brain burst out with these preconceived notions. I brought all my stuff closer and further squeezed myself into the corner. All eyes on the door which illuminated itself every now and then due to the lightning. All other small fears of insects and lizards vanished entirely from my head as there was a bigger fear in front of me, the ultimate fear of death.

'Chhhrrr...' that door opened, my eyes widened, and I put hands over my mouth to suppress my scream. Seconds after, I saw a black structure standing on the jamb of the doorway. Short height, the small structure warranted that it was a child. Lightning flung a sharp flash on his body, and I saw a glimpse of that child. He was naked, and his body had some distinct markings representing some sort of old signs. In the exact moment when lightning let me see what he looked like, it let him see me too. We both realised that we saw each other. Even before I could utter a word, he ran away quickly. My heart came out of my mouth, I swear. I stood up and decided to peep outside the door. I came outside, and raging blaze of the lightning lit up everything for a while. My cabin was surrounded by many of those people. That child hid himself behind one of those men. It was clear that he told his people about my presence in the cabin. They all had some weapon in their hands. Some had spears, some had *trishulas* while others held machetes.

Even before I understood anything, I felt a rough piece of cloth being forcefully put on my head that covered my eyes too.

"Aah… it hurts!!" I shouted but heard nothing in return. I was retaliating, I was hopelessly shouting out loud for some help.

"AAHHH" I screamed as I felt a sharp painful prick on the neck and fell to the ground almost unconsciously. I believe, nothing else was heard from me that night.

17: The Escape

EKLAVYA

I felt a few mild sprinkles of cold water on my face. With great effort, I opened my eyes and saw a glimpse of a unique, vibrant face, so adorable that my eyes felt the warmth of it, making me quickly stand up while maintaining eye contact with the girl. She seemed to be the same age as me and had a bowl in her hand. It was evident that she woke me up by sprinkling water on my face. Before I could wholly immerse myself in the vibrant sight of her, I felt a slight pain in the neck, that instantly made me remember last night's weird and dramatic encounter. I recalled everything that happened last night up until I felt a painful quirk in the neck and fell to the ground.

I was amazed at the magical effect of whatever that made me sleep for the entire last night and half of the next day. The girl looked contented to see me rising to life. She appeared to be one of those bizarre people, but with good behaviour. She looked way better than others, urging a debate inside me whether I should speak with her or not. While that internal conflict was going on, I heard something was being dragged towards the shed in which I was kept. Then two people came in. Huge, horrible and fearless, with a broad net in their hands, they came closer to me. The girl ran out immediately as if she knew what was going to happen but did not want to see it.

"Please don't hit me! I will co-operate!" I pleaded with them. But they did not speak anything, neither did they tranquillise me this time. Seeing me already weak and exhausted they decided not to use that large net to trap me and quickly tied both my hands and feet with ropes that were used for cattle. I wanted to run for my life immediately but found myself without any energy and courage to do so. Moreover, I had nowhere to go, I did not know which way to run and how much to run. Most importantly, the effect of the drug used in that attack influenced my decisions and capabilities. Though I tried to protest but soon subsided as both men were so powerful that my effort was equal to that of a firefly trying to escape the spider web. I was in deep fear as to what was going to happen to me, developing spooky thoughts in my mind. It was natural too. With such torture, sinister thrill and fear of death, how could I keep my thoughts positive and full of hope? Both men pulled me by the rope tied to my waist. I could barely walk and tried persuading them with ease, then I screamed, but due to the difference in our languages, all my words meant nothing and died in vain.

Regardless, I walked with them. Both men dragged me, taking me along the way through their colony. I realised my body carried the same markings and signs as those people had on their bodies. I did not understand anything as to why would those people bother themselves with the creation of markings and signs on my body. By my understanding, I thought of those markings to be poor traditional practice, or it could be something having utmost importance in their culture. Anyone who saw me on the path bounded by those two men followed along. A passer-by acted with his hand, hinting me about getting my throat slit likely. It was then when I felt the ground slipping under my feet. I looked at my death from very near. Those people were likely to witness my horrible death shortly. And I once again thought about my demise.

'Would they chop and separate my head from torso?... or are they going to set me on fire?... They can hang me till death too!... strange thoughts were kicking into my forlorn mind. Shortly afterwards, I saw a square stage where the executioner stood with a big, thick metallic sword in his hand. Besides him, there was a big metallic dong, and a huge wooden throne was right beside the dong. The throne was decorated with animal skin and some bones and had someone giant proudly sitting on it. It appeared as if that person was the king of the tribe. Some people gathered there by that time. Now I was silent. I believed I had no advantage of screaming and retaliating as it was too late. After losing my faith in life and hope in karma, I cooperated with those two men.

The little boy who told his people about me hid in the shed and that beautiful girl who sprinkled water on my face was also there in the crowd. Both seemed to be taking pity on my situation. It became evident from their way of looking at me that they did not want to be a part of whatever was going to happen to me there. Regrets in their eyes for my misfortune was clearly visible. Seeing that remorse in their eyes brought some peace to my mind. Shortly after, the girl and that boy left the scene. All of my intellect, my perspective on life, optimism and courage went away. I felt as if the time passed very slowly and I had decades to remember all pleasant and devastating events from the past. My life flashed before my eyes. It is said that when death approaches, the soul rings a bell before leaving the body and gives one last chance to live the moments of life. I was doing the same, living the moments of my life. But part of my brain was figuring out the way of grabbing the sword from executioner's hand and using it to capture the king. That was the only possible way of getting out of there. My warrior instincts were not letting me give up on my life so easily. Only time could tell if I was going to escape from there or not.

Both men came down right after escorting me to the top of the stage. The giant person sitting on the throne, the executioner and I were present on stage. Others gathered around, watching us. A commotion arose among those people. The executioner put his sword down and quickly picked up a bludgeon, banging it against a nearby metallic dong. A loud resonant sound penetrated the ears of the people, and they became quiet, and all eyes struck on the stage. Everybody witnessed absolute silence there. My ears were completely numb; my brain froze. The executioner saw me with his eyes wide open. His face was emotionless and heart devoid of any feelings. Only if my hands were not tied with the thick rope, I would have picked up the sword that was put down by the executioner on the stage. I stared at the king with my eyes full of questions. As if I was broken from inside not because I was going to die, but because I did not even get a chance to explain everything to the king; that I will die with that weight of not being able to put forth my side of the story. As the king raised his hand, pointing at the executioner, he began to sharpen the edge of the sword for the final showdown. People were convinced that they would witness me dying in front of them, and I was even more certain of my death that day. The talk had started again; the entire tribe was in shock, and so was I. After a while, the executioner stopped sharpening the edge of his sword and waited for the command of the king. As soon as the king ordered, my small, soft neck was in his big strong hand. I fully prepared myself to embrace death and did not resist at all.

Seeing me so calm in a situation like that perhaps put the executioner in deep thinking about what he was going to do. Maybe, he never saw anybody who kept themselves so quiet at the time of their execution. Deep down he was helpless and wasn't ready to kill me, but it was his job to follow the royal orders. He kept my head on the plank designed to chop the flesh of the animals.

'Maa I am coming to meet you, just as you wished in my dream... Let Father and *Amma* know that I am coming to see them!' some last thoughts ran through my mind. I then closed my eyes and waited for the moment when a massive sword would separate my head from the rest of the body.

"What was your reason for intruding into my tribe?" A bold voice was heard by all, and I opened my eyes to the surprise that the king spoke in my language. A new ray of hope awakened within me a few seconds after that.

'At least now I can explain everything to him,' I thought in a sigh.

'Even if I die, I would still be able to release this stress from my soul of not being given a chance to justify myself,' I further pondered.

"Why did you intend to infiltrate into my colony after crossing this dense forest and risking your life? There must be some reason," the king interrogated me, and the executioner released my neck so that I can reply. I stood up, took a few steps towards the king and folded my hands.

"I did not even know about your settlement here. After leaving the cemetery, I went further in the south direction. I saw the jungle upon coming out of such a distance. I was conflicted between making a choice of either going back to the cemetery which was more than five hours of walk and live the same old life or take my chances and enter the jungle and see what was beyond it. And I did not leave the cemetery, the old man and walk for hours just to go back there again. So, I stepped further into the jungle. I somehow managed to stay alive in there. But soon your men found me and brought my prisoned unconscious self here. I did not have any clue that my peaceful existence in the jungle would pose a threat of intrusion to your colony. I am only a child, an ordinary one. I tried my best to understand these people and to explain everything to them, but nobody spoke to me, and nobody knew my language," I explained everything, hoping to get released from their captivity.

"Nice story that was. Do not lie to me!" he said.

"Don't you dare lie to me! I know that you were sent by the corrupt king of Rudraputra state as an undercover who would reveal our location, number, strengths and weaknesses to him so that he could wage a battle and kill us all! He does not want us to live and prosper here. He tried sending his soldiers and agents many times before. Thanks to this mighty jungle, some died in the middle of their journey, and some were killed by us. You see these skins of animals on the throne... we killed them for our protection. Those bones... they belong to those intruders who were caught and killed by my people. This throne will remind us not to fall prey to the people like you! You can't annihilate our colony, nobody can!" he claimed confidently, turned sideways and asked the people in their language that what should be done with the intruder, which in that case was me.

"Ekra ke maar dehi chahi!" (He should be killed!), all of them screamed loudly. I figured that out and was not very optimistic about my chances of survival. The king laughed and waved at the executioner. He, in turn, held my neck again and put me on the stone. I laid down in peace and expected it to end soon and quickly.

Suddenly, a thumping sound emerged from the distance with mixed growling and rumbling noise. It sounded like some people and animals were running together towards the direction of the stage. Moments later, the earth tremored with their vigorous reverberation of steps. Everyone looked surprised and turned around to see what was coming with that tremendous force. The king stood up from the throne, the executioner dropped his sword and walked to the edge of the stage to take a better look. I too quietly stood up and wondered about the source of that roaring sound. Before someone could understand anything and analyse the situation,

"The soldiers of Rudraputra are coming in... We are under attack! Run for your lives!!" someone from the crowd screamed in anxiety, and panic broke out in all the people. They started helter-skelter. Some collided with each other, some fell and were ran over by others, few managed to climb up the stage and reached behind it, while others were clueless about what they should do.

Meanwhile, I was able to untie my hands and thought about picking up the sword again. But there was too much of chaos, and no one cared to keep an eye on me. Seconds after, neighing horses, mooing cows, buffaloes, goats, woofing dogs and all other small and big animals along with the only elephant appeared out from the dust. People were stunned to see their pets running wildly for their freedom. No one had ever thought of such a shocking event. They were simply not prepared to tackle something like that. Some brave-heart men tried catching their animals, some of them succeeded while others lost and saw their cattle running away from them.

TIME

As soon as the raging bustle was gone, all saw the king. The king suddenly looked beside. The executioner stood in shock with his eyes wide opened and in a deliberate search for something, rather someone. People astonishingly stood still, devoid of any reaction on their faces for few seconds. Eklavya was not present on the stage! He vanished, and nobody saw him going. They had no idea what happened and how.

"*Kenne gelle rahli aa?*" (Where were you gone?), the mother asked the little boy.

"*Hiyein rahli aa!*" (Nowhere, I was just here!), he fumbled. Despite being in deep fear and conscious about what he had just witnessed, the little boy had a smile on his face. He knew something that was and would always remain unknown to the rest of the world.

Figure: Animals escaping from the captivity.

18: Fearless Beauty

EKLAVYA

She woke me up from the sleep, saved me from being ruthlessly butchered in front of the entire tribe for I never committed to anything worth getting myself killed that way. And now it had been quite a while since I ran with her in the woods. We sweated profusely after running to the maximum of our capacity. She seemed to know the jungle very well, and upon reaching somewhere safe, sat down to catch her breath. I was tired too. With apparent assurance in my mind that nobody would find us there, I sat beside her. As my breathing became calm, my mind thought of what had just happened. I could not believe what I went through. It was clear that the dramatic stampede of animals and people was not just a coincidence. Instead, it was a plan, a well-executed plan. And I had a firm belief about whose idea was that. I wanted to thank her, but the apparent language barrier could not let me do so.

After some time, we gathered enough stamina to continue our journey. As soon as I stood up, I heard a distant growl and immediately looked at her, realising there was some animal nearby. Her survival instinct kicked in naturally. After running for my life for hours, I again found myself trapped in danger. I thought who could possibly find me in that dense jungle, but I forgot about the wild animals. It made me wonder if I was really a source of bad luck. The roar seemed to be coming closer with each passing second. I saw a stash of wood logs and instantly picked up two thick and long logs to be used as a weapon against whatever approached us. As the sound became clearer, I came to know it was a bear. My fear tripled! How could I have fought with a bear alone? I had no clue if that girl was strong enough to combat a bear. But I had no option but to give in all I had to save her and myself from being killed. My heart pounded heavily so much so that I heard it throbbing. Besides having basic knowledge of the scriptures, I believed I had developed few combat skills too. I learnt to fight in *Gurukul* and honed my skills over the years spent in the cemetery. Cutting the trees for wood, digging in the land and other daily activities boosted my physical strength. Now it was time for me to use my training given to me by *Acharya* Virbhadra to protect her and myself from that monster. While I planned on my strategy and prepared myself mentally and physically to take on that bear, I saw the girl already equipped with her weapon in position. Her attacking gesture warranted that she knew how to fight. I was a bit relieved and drew confidence from her. Rattling in plants and bushes grew, and the roar became louder.

Suddenly, a big brown bear came out of the bushes. It lifted its broad head to sniff the air, and it was spitting streaks of saliva. Within moments, it caught the whiff of us both standing not so far away from it. The bear saw us and bounded at a surprising pace. Its eyes were fixed on the girl and me, making me scream loudly. I ran towards the bear with all the power and force. It jumped and smashed me on the face, and I lost my balance, falling to the ground. My face seemed to be covered in blood as the ground turned red after I fell on it. Then the bear charged at the girl. She ducked and stabbed her wood log in the face of the bear. It again swiped at her, spraying its own blood everywhere. It became fiercer and mauled her hand with its mouth. She screamed, she cried in immense pain. I, laying on the ground in pain saw all that. My eyes go wide, and my warrior instinct released a boost in my body. I couldn't see her dying in front of me. She saved my life and now it was time for me to help her save hers. I stood up and charged at the bear from behind. It released her hand and turned up to me. For a moment, I thought I was better lying on the ground. Meanwhile, she stabbed her weapon in the eye of the bear. Without waiting for a second, I nudged the wooden branch into bear's mouth. Blood poured from its eyes and mouth. It ran away in distress, leaving behind both of us, severely wounded and semi-conscious. We groaned in pain.

That encounter with my potential death for a few seconds was the longest passing time of my life, and I am sure it was her worst nightmare too. She quickly stood up somehow and used a small chunk of fabric to cover her wound in hand. Then she rushed towards me, put some leaves on my face and tied it with another chunk of same cloth.

"Nectar of leaves will heal your wounds... it is going to be alright... these are just a few scratches!!" she said. Hearing her speak in my language pulled me out of the semi-conscious state I was in. I forgot all my pain for a moment as a sheer surprise after listening to the girl took over me.

"You knew my language!! You can talk...Why did you not say anything so far?" I asked her.

"I was not sure if you were sent by the enemies or genuinely stuck in the jungle that night. I had to make sure you were clean," she replied.

"Moreover, if I had talked to you there, we both would be dead!" she further added.

"So what made you think I am clean now?" I showed a little frustration.

"I believe you were genuinely stuck in the jungle that night. Had you been mere a spy, you would have revealed your identity in the hope that they would spare your life. Also, the dart that hit you in the neck makes people speak the truth as well. All you said that night while under the influence of the drug was 'Maa... I am coming to meet you... Maa, tell father and *Amma* too! They deemed me as sullied... Maa... I am coming to meet you!' Nobody could get their heads around to what you said and why. No intruder had said so in the past. They all had to accept who they were," she explained.

"My brother told me about your condition when he saw you in the cabin. I knew you were mistaken as some intruder. I could not let you die there. In the hope that you will be saved, Brother and I released all the animals, and it worked!" she continued.

TARA

"I can't thank you enough for your help. You are courageous, just as Pundir was," he hugged me in gratitude. I didn't see that coming, and without wondering about who Pundir was, I let him hug me. Electric tingles in my body rushed as it was for the first time someone held me in their arms. His sinewed and muscular body rubbed against the silky white cloth I was draped in. Sweat from his chiselled bare chest soaked into the fabric around my ample bosom, making my skin partially visible. I did not want him to get his arms off my body, but at the same time, I knew a few more seconds would grow triggers of sexual desires inside me.

"Rudraputra is not very far from here. Let's keep walking, and soon we will enter the capital," I suggested, muzzling my feelings and controlling myself from falling for his physique.

"I don't know your name," he said.

"Neither do I!" I countered, and we mildly laughed, gasping and moaning in pain.

"I am Eklavya, the son of Vyas and scion of Ikshvaku," he said with pride.

"I am Tara. I don't remember who my parents were. I am alone in this world," I introduced myself, recalling my past that brought a tinge of sadness on my face.

"But you just said he was your brother," Eklavya recalled.

"The tribal people found me in this jungle. My parents abandoned me when I was small, maybe five or six! It was obvious that I wasn't an intruder or a spy, so they adopted me. Since then I was living with them. But certainly, I am not one of them," I told him.

"Now that you have escaped from there, greatness awaits you," he tried to motivate me. We resumed walking for another few hours. Eklavya shared his life story with me, in return, I shared mine with him. I never realised when I started imagining my future with him during our escape from the jungle to reach Rudraputra. It was probably too quick to fall for him, but I had no control over my feelings. He was a caring man. I didn't know if he had the same feelings as I had for him.

The forest was primordial and didn't seem to end. Grains of sticky gels were covering the malady-brown trunks of alpine trees. The raw paths were filled with mud, stones, forks, trees, leaves, insects, worms and what not. Eklavya's facial bandage was damp and fragmented. My arm was sore, and pus was oozing from the wound. Both of us, no matter how much exhausted we were, kept on walking as we feared another and probably our very last encounter with wild creatures. Seemed as if the bear encounter was an incident waiting to just happen. The rotting air and smothering climate gave the ideal dwelling place to those who worshipped the *Kali*. The dusk was setting in. We heard the chirping of the birds flying back to their nests. I felt a sudden decrease in temperature. The wind started to blow faster. Howling sounds ghosted through the trees. Whether it was from the predator or the prey, only jungle could tell. Dense forest would let itself into the dark quite sooner than rest of the landscapes. As both of us starved, we ate a few wild berries that left us with the same sickening taste of gore. It was a forest to be avoided.

"We are right there... just don't stop!" I said.

"I don't want to spend one more night in this jungle," he testified. We both were thirsty, hungry and in beat-up condition. It became hard for him to catch up to my speed. I, however, was confident about the city not being far from where we were. Eklavya lost his hope, he asked if we could take some rest.

"Look! The trail has started now... trees and bushes are disappearing with the distance ahead! You know what it means?" I asked him in excitement, hoping that it would encourage him to keep walking and it worked.

"Yes! We made it! The city is not far away now. Let's keep on going," he suggested with enthusiasm. After a few minutes, I saw some flashing points of light. Some were yellow while others were white.

"Those are the lamps and candles inside the huts. Do you see those cabins, Eklavya?" I asked.

"Yes, I see them," he replied.

"We have entered the outskirts of the city. We can die in peace here. At least, we would not be someone's food. I was scared to the core after seeing that bear," I confessed.

"Me too. But you fought like a warrior. I was amazed!" he appreciated.

There were some shelters and huts ahead. We reached there and knocked some doors. Some people opened the door for us but did not offer any help, some simply did not open the door while others shouted from inside and told us to leave right there right then. I was disappointed with the kind of treatment both of us received. My expectations from this world died in vain.

"May God give them the vision to lead a life of a human," Eklavya prayed. We were thirsty and drank some water from the well nearby and prepared ourselves to spend the night outside. I was still at ease for we were not in the jungle anymore. Tremendous exhaustion took over my body. The last thing I heard that night was Eklavya's guttural snores, and I never realised when I fell asleep.

19: Master of All Trades

EKLAVYA

"Hey! Get up, wake up! Get up…!" few nudges by someone woke me up. Upon opening my eyes, I saw a woman leaning beside me.

"Who are you? I have never seen you here before… Where have you come from?" she asked.

"I lost my way… aah!" my face hurt, laden with some deep dark-red welts on my right cheek. I, upon touching it, winced as the wound swirled without mercy. The pain was deep and warm but in an undesired way.

'I wish I could end my life right here. But I was born to serve a greater purpose, and I must live to do that,' I thought and groaned and saw another woman rushed to bring first aid for both of us while I continued.

"I was lost in the woods. I came from my village in the South direction on the shore of the Ganges. My friend Tara brought us here," I said while pointing out at Tara. She was still sleeping, looking even more beautiful than ever. In that very moment, I wished I could take her wounds and pain on me and give her the love she had been deprived of since her childhood.

"Did you knock at the door last night?" the woman asked.

"Yes! We did. We were in dire need of some food and first aid for both of us. We knocked on everybody's door in the neighbourhood but realised it was the wrong place in wrong time for us. No one offered any help," I said with a decent smile on my thrashed face.

"It was a matter of great surprise to us that no one came out nor did anybody help," I further added.

TARA

Their conversation fell into my ears, and I woke up in a snap. After listening to Eklavya, tears came out of that woman's eyes.

"Why are you crying? Please forgive my words. I did not mean to hurt you in any way. Please don't cry!" Eklavya showed his concern.

"Please don't apologise. You have done nothing wrong. Last night brought a storm of hardships for all of us. Seems like we have to live with it for the rest of our lives," she said.

"I did not get you. What hardship are you talking about?" I asked while inspecting my wounded arm. The mud and grit had become enmeshed with raw pink flesh from my right elbow to my hand. It was going to be very painful to clean that wounded arm. I looked at Eklavya who was already staring at my arm in agony. Somewhere deep inside, he blamed himself for my condition.

"Last night, hill bandits attacked our village before you came here. This is not new for us. They have been killing and taking our domestic animals for their food. They have been robbing our valuables, groceries and whatnot since ages," the woman explained. Eklavya listened to her with sheer surprise.

"This settlement of ours is very far from the capital region of Rudraputra. So, we have been left alone by the administration. Bandits live in these forests surrounding us. Whenever they run out of their supplies, they attack us and take it all from here forcibly. The corrupt king of Rudraputra has done nothing about it despite being told about this issue so many times in the past. He is lost in majestic pleasures and has turned into a monster. We are hopeless and helpless now. Thus, we all decided not to retaliate and surrender everything to those dacoits so that there would be no violence. We want peace in our village," the woman further explained to us.

My sleep vanished completely after listening to her. I empathised with the woman. Meanwhile, people gathered around us three. Everyone had the same question regarding our whereabouts.

"My name is Eklavya. I am the son of Vyas and banished scion of Ikshvaku clan. My people abandoned me as they claim I am cursed. It is me who lost his mother, *Amma* and father. I lost my village, my *Gurukul* and my childhood. And yet I am cursed and unholy for them. What did they lose? I have come from a village situated on the banks of the Ganges in the south direction, and she is my friend Tara. We both have no one in this world whom we could call ours. It was us last night who knocked on your doors. I must apologise to all of you for that," Eklavya confessed and folded his hands together. I did the same.

"No! No... don't ask for apologies. You are our guests now. We are embarrassed for not being able to come out and help you. We were afraid and disturbed," someone said from the crowd. Some people assisted us with bandages, herbs and medicinal pastes the other woman brought for the treatment of our wounds.

"It is definitely a crime to oppress others. But letting someone oppress you holds an equal amount of persecution. And you don't make peace by letting evil flourish," Eklavya said while looking at the woman who said something about peace just a moment ago. She pondered what she had said.

"None of you have done anything ever to sacrifice all your belongings, cattle and most importantly your freedom to those hooligans. You don't owe them anything! Do you?" He stood up in the middle of his face treatment and took charge. His pain was all gone, and there was a charm in his voice as if he was all prepared to lead those innocent people. Silence prevailed all over, and people listened to him with all their spirits. I too looked at him agape and for a moment, could not believe it was the same person who was about to be butchered previous day, feeling proud of my plan and for showing the courage of saving his life. It was worth the risk. I smiled gently.

"What are you people afraid of?... their weapons, their numbers?? Are you scared of losing your life? Your life, like this, is not worth living anyway. Don't you want to protect what's yours? Your rights? What is holding you back... Don't you trust in your abilities and powers? Why don't you speak now! Someone tell me now! Are you all dead inside?" he shouted in desperation.

"The time has come that you all play the role of being a *Kshatriya*," commanded Eklavya.

"But we are not *Kshatriyas*. All those who were, are now in King's army," someone said in the crowd.

"Huh! What do you mean, gentleman? Seems to me like the education system in your village is broken too, just as your will to fight for your rights is!" he expressed regret. The lady who woke up Eklavya began explaining,

"We did not get that. It has been rightly said that those who belong from *Kshatriya* social order joined the King's army. They fight wherever and whenever the King orders them to fight."

Meanwhile, food was brought for us. I salivated at the sight of it. Eklavya too was eager to hog it. The joy of eating staved off all our pains for a moment. Eklavya continued while eating,

"Man was categorised in four *varnas* (social orders) by his work and not caste or religion. Those who impart knowledge and help others with traditional rites and rituals are *Brahmins*. Those who administer and fight for the greater good and lead others to prosperity are *Kshatriyas*. The one who does business and trade is

Vaishya. While those who engage in the service of others are *Shudras*. There shall be no comparison between each class, no class must have greater privilege than the other for it is our work that has been categorised and not us as humans," he educated everyone collectively.

People were mesmerised by the way he spoke, enlightening them.

"Those soldiers and their king are nothing more than puppets, they are not at all *Kshatriyas*. Instead, they are coward! The time has come that now you people should also perform your *Kshatriya* dharma, there is no need for you to sit on the trust of that crafty and senseless king," he further added.

"You are right, son! We should have stood up for our rights and freedom long before this. But it's not too late yet. Now that we have you by our side, we will conquer this too!" said the lady in optimism. And there arose a discussion on what Eklavya had just said to those people. They all shared their thoughts with each other. Some seemed enthusiastic, some not so happy, some did not care while a handful of people were not in favour of letting a stranger be their mentor and guide. Eklavya had an idea that not everyone would easily join their hands to tackle this stubborn problem. Adopting a change is difficult sometimes.

"I believe you are much more in numbers than those bandits," he broke their murmuring.

"Yes, we are. But we don't know how to fight with those bandits. They are brutal, they know how to use their weapons, and they are merciless," someone brought that to everyone's notice.

"We will teach you how to fight! Only if you are willing to learn from your soul," I said.

"You can always become brutal and show no mercy to those who don't deserve it. Are we on par with them now!?" Eklavya counter-argued. No one spoke any further.

"We will design our own tools, equipment and weapons and learn how to use them. Adults, kids, elderly, males and females everybody will be trained. Tara will pay particular attention to girls and women. She can teach you very well. I have seen her fighting. She must have got a warrior's blood running through her veins," he assured everyone while looking at me. I was amazed upon seeing his faith in me, and I nodded my head in affirmative. My love for him became even profound.

"Working adults will learn before they leave for their works in the morning. Non-working men and women will be trained after they finish their household works. Teenagers will be taught after they come back from their school. And elders can decide for themselves," proposed Eklavya.

"We thought we all will be trained together," said that women.

"No! There is a reason why I said that. Working adults will first learn how to fight and then practice it every day before they leave for their job. This will let them put their energy and zeal into the training. They would not have any motivation and energy left in them after work. Even if they get a little tired during their training in the morning, they still would have to go to work as there are bigger motivations and necessity to earn for their survival. Non-working men and women, on the other hand, would finish their primary household work like cooking, cleaning and any other work they do so that families don't get affected as a whole and keep on functioning. Teenagers will learn how to fight after they come back from the *Gurukul*. Energy is not a concern for them. However, they need to be at their schools with a fresh mind and a relaxed body. They can practice afterwards, but their education shall not be affected at any cost. Elders can decide for themselves," he finished talking and sat down again. Those who were dressing up his face continued to do so. Everyone appreciated his reasoning skills and determination.

After discussing among each other about whether they should trust his plan or not, almost everyone agreed to take a stand against those bandits.

"We are with you Eklavya! We must learn how to fight, we are with you!" they all shouted collectively. Eklavya was puffed merrily. He was happy that people were ready to accept the change and determined to do something for their betterment. Perhaps he also knew that a handful of those who were against his ideas would join him soon.

"Alright then! From tomorrow, we will implement our plan and start making weapons and tools. I would need wood logs, metallic scrapers, farming equipment, household stuff, anything and everything you think could be used as a weapon. I will teach some volunteers how to make weapons from household stuff and farming equipment. It would take another month for those bandits to come again here. We will be all ready to defend ourselves and if needed, to attack them too," Eklavya assured.

"Why don't you join us in the *Gurukul* whenever you get a chance? You too can teach students," someone came up front and suggested him. Everybody else supported his suggestion.

"Our kids can learn a lot from you Eklavya. Please do us this small favour and give some of your time to them as well," they all requested.

"I will teach them per the best of my knowledge and belief for sure," he agreed, and a wave of contentment ran all over the place.

"Long live Eklavya! Long live the scion of Ikshvaku!" People cherished him.

The village went back to its regular routine. Some left for work, kids went to *Gurukul*, most women left for their homes, the elderly sat together to have some chit-chat, and

Eklavya and I thought about preparing the plan of action. There was a hope in everybody's heart, the hope of getting their freedom and living lives without any fear. Everybody geared up themselves for the upcoming big day.

20: The Bad News

TARA

The next morning, the working class as planned, gathered in the field nearby before heading towards their workplaces. Eklavya was already present there with me. We brought many wooden sticks, some spears and some bamboo logs in front of them and asked those people to pick whatever they liked. There were few iron chains as well. They all picked up one weapon of their choice and stood side by side. Their enthusiasm to turn themselves into warriors was clearly visible. Eklavya began with teaching them about the possession of the weapon. He showed them how to hold their weapons. After doing some light movements, he asked them to always move and repeat that move until they become perfect in it, carefully monitoring everybody's workout and correcting them if they did anything wrong. People were learning it with full zeal and showed their passion. Some were quite good in one to one combat, but they did not know that before. After an hour or so of practice, Eklavya gave them permission to go.

Those who were not working joined next. That group had mostly women in it. I asked them to bring whatever they deem fit for a weapon from their house. Many carried knives, some had utensils and remaining brought torn clothes from their homes. I made one thing clear to them that the spirit of the fight is all in mind. If they are willing to fight, they can turn an ordinary thing into a deadly weapon. Everybody understood that and began following what I said. As women already mastered the art of holding knives in their hands, I only had to teach them how to use it on vital parts of the human body and soon realised women were far more efficient than men were. Their years-long practice of using domestic items on a daily routine had made them very good at it.

After women were done with their training, old people expressed their desire to learn. Eklavya and I had a plan of using elderlies to divert the minds of the bandits. That would buy some time for those people to prepare against the bandits. Now the children had also come back from their schools. Eklavya asked the teenagers to bring their playing stuff like marbles, balls, bats and whatever they had with them and taught them how to use those things in an attack. It was not a big deal for those kids to learn. After a few days of regular practice, Eklavya and I shortlisted some of the best and active learners and made them supervisors of their groups. This made sure everyone got proper attention during their training.

TIME

One day, the king of Rudraputra wanted to go hunting in the jungle. Killing animals was one of his hobbies, and he never felt any guilt while murdering innocent animals just for his amusement. He was accompanied by some of his soldiers, ministers and spies. While on his way to the jungle he arrived in the village where he saw people perfectly synchronised with each other and practising with their weapons. His eyes located Eklavya and Tara soon. Seeing those people united for a common purpose took him by surprise, and he asked his ministers about what was going on there. Ministers said it was some foreigner giving self-defence training to those poor people. The king toyed with that idea and moved ahead for his hunt. However, he ordered one of his spies to keep an eye on every activity of that foreigner who was none other than Eklavya.

The training continued for a few more days, and gradually ordinary people became skilled at one to one land combat. Those who did not want Eklavya to be their mentor also came to him requesting them to be allowed to learn the art of fighting. They clearly saw improvements in fellow villagers. Eklavya also included them in the group. As days went by, almost everyone in the village turned into a fighter. They sometimes got nervous, but then relying on their learned skills, they soon regained their courage to fight for their freedom.

It was about to be a month since the bandits attacked the village. People were anxious, concerned and cautious about them attacking again. Though they had been practising the art of combat since past so many days, their fear of death did not let them utilise their full potential. It was then when Eklavya decided to put an end to their training and let them decide what was best for them. The next day, when everyone gathered in the same field, he announced the completion of their training. He also suggested them to ponder upon what they were going to do. In case if anyone was doing it under pressure, he advised them not to take part in the battle. Villagers did not spend so many days training themselves for saying no to the combat. They badly wanted their freedom from the torture of those hill bandits. Thus, they all kept on practising without receiving any instructions from Eklavya and Tara. Eklavya was happy to see their confidence in themselves. And Tara was glad to see Eklavya happy.

EKLAVYA

The day was quickly swirled, and the night sky gulped the sun entirely. After my regular meeting with the villagers in the evening, I sat at the *choupal* whereas, everybody retreated to their homes. Tara had some household work left to do with fellow women, so she went with them. The sky was devoid of any stars, and it appeared to be the night of the new moon. I laid on the *choupal*, looking up at the dead sky and embracing its darkness. I believed that great things often come out from complete obscurity. I remembered that night in the forest when I was lost in sleep by looking at the bright skies. Not thinking much about the future, I remembered some good old days. I was filled with different kinds of emotions arising in my heart at the same time as I had seen some excellent and some terrible days in my small life that made me quite mature at a very young age.

I also thanked Mohammad once again for not letting me die in the Ganges a few years ago. Had he not arrived there in time, I would have been dead long ago. I smiled at the puzzling course of his destiny, wondering what the old man was possibly doing for all those days. I recalled my initial years spent with *Amma* and Father.

As I remembered that dream of Maa, my eyes became wet, and tears rolled out of them. The one who taught others to live life without fear, became himself weak and vulnerable that night. The fear of losing my people haunted me. I did not want any of those innocent people to die in the battle. But there was no way I could be sure about that. I knew that even if I asked them to give up on the fight, they would refuse my request. People cultivated sheer faith in their efforts and skills by that time. They developed unshakable trust in my training much like the way I had faith in *Acharya* Virbhadra's training. Everyone had a hope in their hearts of getting rid of those bandits forever. I knew that upon being refused to comply with them, the bandits will do whatever they would seem to be right to get hold of the people. And indeed, there was no possible way of getting everything right on track without retaliating and revolution. It was too late for me to turn away that fiasco. Those innocent beings had already won their battle with hill bandits in their minds. All they had to do was to win it in reality.

The night became even dense, and I was still lost in the false world of memories. Thinking about some unsolved mysteries in life my head tore itself apart due to the stress. After trying so hard and for so many times, I found myself failing to connect some broken strings together. Maybe I was just too young to deal with the fate and understand karma's game altogether. I couldn't know the higher purpose of my life yet. The sequence of strange events forced me to think and rethink the laws of karma, kismet and cosmic balance. I applied all the reasoning and logic that *Acharya* Bhushan taught me, but it didn't help much. Seemed as if the mighty playwright wanted me to suffer and struggle for the entire life in search of the purpose of realising true self. An extended and elaborated introspection came to an end as my body and mind were tired. My eyes bore the weight of exhaustion, and they started drowning in the lap of sleep. I was given shelter by the villagers to sleep and decided to go inside the shed.

As soon as I stood up and stepped towards it, I heard something. Something came nearer with each passing second and in blazing speed. It was so dark that I could not figure out who was running towards me. Even before I could think of anything, the rain sharpened the smells of smoke and earth. I only momentarily saw the movement when the unknown crossed by the windows lit with lanterns. At one time, I thought of screaming and let everyone know about the attack of the bandits. But the question of being completely wrong and waking up the entire neighbourhood from their peaceful, serene sleep stopped me from taking that chance. 'Bandits would anyway wake these people up,' I thought and didn't do much about it.

I geared up with my sword-like weapon to make the first substantial hit on the enemy. Steps became crisp and closer; my breath became faster, eyes widened double to its size. I sensed a thrill, a lot massive than what I felt while confronting that bear in the jungle as Tara was not there to help me in that fight now. Few shrubberies got stirred, and I ran ahead of them to attack whatever was there, but soon realised it was some small animal roaming inside the bushes in desperation. As I took a deep breath in a sigh, I felt someone patting on my shoulder. I removed that hand and swept my sword in the air in a snap.

"Hey! Hold on… take it easy!" said the person. He was restless and taking partial breaths.

"Who are you??" I asked him in doubt.

"I came from the cemetery. The old man is in a critical condition. He thinks he might not live for long. He wants to meet you in his final days. Please go and see him before it's too late!" he told me. I stood still for a while after listening to that stranger.

"What's your name?... How did you know that I was here...?" I asked in anxiety.

"We have met with each other for so many times now. The clock is ticking Eklavya… time is precious for him and for you too… Go on, go there!!" he shouted and ran away in an unknown direction.

"Hey! Listen…STOP!!" I shouted, but he did not stop.

Figure: Bear approaching Eklavya & Tara.

21: The Dilemma

EKLAVYA

I sweated profusely and could not understand what to do next, somehow settling my mind to go visit the old man. I rushed to Tara to inform her about my immediate dismissal for the cemetery.

"Tara! Tara... open the door!" I shouted while making loud thuds on the door. The door opened after a while.

"What happened!? Is everything alright!?" she asked in worry.

"Tara, I have to go to the cemetery now! Its caretaker is not well, and he is seeking my presence. I must leave now!" I briefly explained to her.

"It's pouring heavily. It would not be safe for you to cross the jungle now! And how do you know that the caretaker is really not well and needs you to be there??" she suggested and asked.

"I don't know Tara! Someone just told me about his serious health condition," I replied.

"What if it is a hoax? What if someone is trying to fool you into their trap??" she suggested possible outcomes.

"What if he is actually taking his last breaths? What if it is not a trap... I don't have much time to think about all this. All I know is I am leaving now!" I informed her.

"Wait! I will come with you," she said.

"No! You will stay with them. They need your help and support here more than I will need it there. I will be fine! Don't worry about me," I said while turning around.

"Okay take this with you. It will be of some use to you in the journey," she handed me a knife and a bag filled with some food and water.

"I will come back as soon as I can. Don't go anywhere without me!" I said and left immediately.

"May God be with you!" wished Tara and she shut the door. I knew she might have laid down in the bed soon after I left, but sleep wouldn't come easily to her that night.

I almost ran towards the jungle. I walked with my full capacity and as fast as I could. My vision and pace were limited due to heavy downpouring, but that did not stop me from moving ahead. The old man nurtured me like a father. He saw me grow from a teenager into an adult. He helped me when no one else was there to take care of me. He was a teacher, caretaker, employer, friend and a well-wisher to me. Then how could I just not go see him during his final days? Such a profound relationship flourished between two of us. I hoped to see him as fit as he was before my departure from the cemetery. My feet and arms were scratched off by the thorny bushes and shrubberies. I stepped ahead on the trail with immense pain and difficulty. Besides being worried about the old man's condition, I wondered about who that unknown person was. His words circulated tirelessly in my mind. 'Who was he? And how come he came to me in such a sudden instance?' I pondered. 'Even he (the old man) did not know anyone other than me. Then how he sent that person to me without even knowing where I was...' I was trying to get my questions answered but could not get my head around that. 'And then why did that person say that he has met with me many times before? I never saw him or knew him before.' I further wondered in my head. Those questions kept returning to my subconscious. I was not sure if I could ever get the answers to those questions.

Few hours passed by, the rain had stopped. I was tired after running and walking for several hours. Then, I almost ran out of energy and many times thought of taking some rest. But I knew stopping would kill the valuable time the old man had. So, I kept on walking, at a slower pace though. It was dawn at that point. The sun had not risen yet. But everything was clearly visible to me. I knew I headed in the right direction. The cemetery was not far from there. I was hungry too and quickly ate the food while on the move. I saw the pathway after some time. That induced a boost in my body. As I increased the pace, my heart became heavy and more cumbersome with the assumptions of what I might witness at the cemetery. I tried to stay positive and optimistic but couldn't. Bad ideas and undesired notions filled my mind with anxiety. I saw the iron gates of the cemetery. It seemed as if nothing had changed outside of the cemetery since I left. And I wished nothing changed inside the cemetery too. I opened the rusty gates, and a loud squeaky sound emerged. There was nothing different about it. But I felt something strange in the air inside the compound. I walked swiftly through the graveyard and saw the hut. The lantern still glowed with its flames dim. 'Probably, he forgot to blow off the light,' I thought. The wooden door was already opened as usual. It was in even worse condition. 'I knew he would not repair this door ever,' I gave it a thought, entering inside and saw the old man lying on the floor. I had a hunch of what had happened to him.

"Wake up! I am home… See I am here… I told you I would come! Wake up now!!" I tried waking him up only to find that he was no more.

"Oh! Come on!! I told you to wait for me. I told you I would come to meet you! You should not have let me go that evening! It's all your fault… are you listening?? It's all your goddamn fault!!" I said but got no response from him, and his body kept on lying on the floor. I sat beside the dead body and cried immensely.

"I am sullied indeed! Whoever came closer to me got death! Why!? Why would you do that to me!! What have I done to deserve this kind of fate?!" I screamed in dejection.

"Whoever will know my story will have their faith in you destructed! Ever since I gained consciousness, I have been worshipping you like anything! In peace… in fierceness… with satisfaction… and in distress… amid days and at evenings too! I have given my profitable time and commitment to you... Did I ever ask for anything in return? Did I? Have I at any point undermined you? I know the appropriate response is NO! Why aren't you talking to me... You fake... You are false! Is this what you provide for your devotees consequently? The eternal silence... The invalidated expectation... Tell me if you are fake or genuine? Where are you? Where would I be able to see you? Do you ever talk? I see no you! I doubt your reality! Are you listening? I question your reality... You unreal being, prove me wrong if you can! Will you ever prove me wrong? Disclose to me that you exist... Can you? Huh... you can't! Since you are nothing, you are nowhere! I, Eklavya, the son of Vyas and the scion of Ikshvaku, disregard your reality... deny your existence! I cease to acknowledge you! You, the purported god-like! Go to damnation you fake... I see no you!" I screamed and cursed the God in anger. I laid on the floor beside the dead old man and continued wailing. There was nothing else I could do.

TIME

Those who have taken birth must die. Even reincarnations of almighty himself and his prophets had to leave this world after accomplishing their central goal on earth. Then what audacity did the old man have to escape the only truth in this world? What could Eklavya possibly do to revert that death? Nothing! All he could do was get over the past and prepare himself to lead his future life. After losing himself in remorse for several hours, Eklavya had no tears left in his eyes. His face was numb, and eyes swelled.

He realised it was evening, and he had to bury the dead body too. He saw outside the cemetery if someone could help him in the burial of the old man. Nobody was there to be seen. Eklavya lifted the dead body himself and brought it to the graveyard, remembering some words of the old man,

'My life is withering away with each passing day. I wish to rest in peace right here, next to my beloved wife in this grave... Buying space here in this barren land is becoming more and more expensive. Better safe than sorry, I reserved my spot! Haha!' He never imagined that such time would come soon when he would fulfil the old man's desire to be buried right next to his wife. Eklavya put the dead body in the same grave dug by the old man himself a few months ago. He only had to dig it up to some extent. After putting the body in the grave, he covered and levelled it with the soil. He was surprised to witness that the one who assisted many with their burial and cremation in the past was himself helpless that day. Nobody came to his funeral. Seemed like he already knew that he will be left alone and thus, dug his own grave in advance. The only regret Eklavya had was not being able to reach there in time. He would never be able to know what the old man wanted to share with him or say to him in his last days.

Eklavya was done with the honourable burial of the old man, and by then the night took over the day. He came inside the hut and entered the old man's room. He found a paper scribbled with something on it that made him overwhelmed with feelings. The letter said,

'Life halted after you left. Mornings aren't refreshing anymore, neither evenings remained vibrant. I was alone, I am alone, and I will be alone forever. I never feared to be alone. But, since you left me, loneliness is all that kills me from inside. There is no one to talk to, no one to share my feelings with and nowhere to go to. Seems as if I lost my family once again. It is too much for a single life to hold on to. I have made myself understand that you may never come again to see me. But I could not believe that I lost you forever. Seems like I have to spend the rest of my life waiting for you to come back to this cemetery. I will need you for sure, if not for anything else then to get myself buried under the earth. Would you lend me a hand for one last time, just as you did for the past five years? Don't forget to give the charge of the cemetery to someone like you. It has been my home for the past five decades, it has been your home for five years too, so don't abandon it just like that. If possible, repair the door too. May God bless you. I think I will not be able to see you now. I will tell your mother and father that you are doing great in life. And don't worry I would not say a thing about *Maha-Purohit*'s horrible deeds. This is the end of me. Ameen!'

Now Eklavya had to arrange for someone who could take care of the cemetery. He could not leave everything just like that. And so, he spent the night in the graveyard, hoping to find someone to manage the cemetery the next day. He blew off the lantern and surrendered himself to the world of trance. 'Kill them! Attack!... Do it as Eklavya told us...We will take what's ours from these bandits. Tara! Give me that spear!... Capture their horses... Don't let them run away tonight! Kill them!!' Eklavya silently witnessed everything. He saw his people in the village fought courageously with those bandits. This strong reaction and the level of preparation of the villagers took those bandits by surprise, and they were failing to defend themselves. As a result, some of them were killed by the people, some got serious injuries while remaining ran away for their lives. Seemed like the villagers got their freedom from those monsters. Tara stood at a distance and had a smile on her face. 'You did it! they made it!!' she said to Eklavya. 'AAhhhh...Huh...h..u..h' he woke up in the middle of the night from his dream. 'Oh! Lord, may what I just saw in the dream turn into reality.' He prayed and soon remembered his words of denial to His (God's) presence. He nodded his head sideways on his childish behaviour and slept again.

Eklavya woke up early in the morning and went to take a bath in Ganga. After returning from the shore, he went into the nearby community and asked if someone would take care of the cemetery. Nobody agreed initially. It was then when he told them that all the money they would make will go in their pocket, some men took the responsibility. He quickly showed them the cemetery and told them about how to proceed with the rituals. He took a minute to stand near the grave of the old man and bid his final farewell to him. Completely unaware of what he was about to witness next, Eklavya retreated towards the village where he left off Tara with other people.

22: The Biggest Mistake

EKLAVYA

It was again several hours of the journey on foot. I, being at ease and thinking what wrong could happen now, followed the ground trail that passed through the trees and vegetation in the jungle. I knew I almost reached the village, and strongly desired to meet the villagers as soon as possible to know how everything was. Moreover, I eagerly wanted to know how Tara was. With each step taken into the village, I came close to a man sitting on the ground in absolute silence. The immense pain was visible on his face. Seemed as if he lost his senses to the trauma he was suffering from. I never saw him in the village before. For the sake of humanity, I asked if everything was alright with him. But he did not even bother to listen to me. Or apparently, he was not able to attend to me due to the lack of focus and interest. It appeared to me as if he was lost in deep remorse. Not paying much attention to him and his condition, I proceeded straight to where Tara was staying with other women.

On my way, I saw nobody. Streets were devoid of any movement, be it transit or humans. There was an unearthly silence in the village that dusk. As it was late evening already, I thought everyone must be inside their house. People there and in every village for that matter would go to bed soon after the sunset as they wake up early in the morning. Some left their house even before the sunrise. Also, they felt safe and secure by being inside their homes. Remaining outside in the night left them vulnerable to wild animals and most importantly to the bandits. I, upon reaching Tara's house knocked on the door, but nobody came out.

'Tara...Tara!!' I called her name while knocking hard on the door, but nobody spoke anything, neither the door opened. In desperation, I pushed the door little harder, only to discover it was already unlocked from inside. I rushed inside and found no one in the house. It took me by sheer surprise as it never happened in the past month that someone kept their door unlocked and left the house unattended. Villagers kept their doors locked all the times to safeguard their belongings from being robbed. I ran into another house and found nobody was inside there as well. The door was opened to my surprise, making me a little worried then. I still remembered the dream I saw last night, and it recalled itself to my mind like an alarm to what might have happened there.

"No! No! No!!" I blabbered in nervousness and ran back all the way to that person I had seen sitting weirdly on the ground.

"What has happened to you?? Why do I not see anyone except you in the village?" I asked him in anxiety. In return, I got nothing but the same dull face, sad and shock-filled eyes and utter silence from the man.

"Why don't you speak to me! Where is everyone?? Tell me now!!" I shouted at him, but he still sat like a statue. With a hope that I could bring him out of the shock, I nudged him tremendously and rubbed his neck. In desperation, I slapped tightly on that man's cheeks.

"Tell me where is everybody?? Did the bandits attack?!" I asked again, but politely. He was out of his shock momentarily. As soon as he gained his conscious, he cried vehemently. I watched him agape and apologised for slapping him. That man was afraid of the turmoil that was wrenching him from inside.

"Don't kill me! Please Don't kill me... I will not tell the king about you! Please don't kill me!" he lost control of his faculties and had gone mentally unstable. I suspected that he saw something very perplexed and sinister.

"I will not kill you, I promise! Just tell me where everyone is? I will not ask again!! Where. Is. Everyone?" I stressed my question to him. And then he pointed his finger in a direction, crying immensely again. His finger pointed towards a pond nearby. I rushed towards it without waiting for a second. I reached there and what I saw blew my mind completely. I puked immediately after seeing the floating dead swollen body of the woman who woke me up on the very first morning in the village. I looked back to the man hoping to call him for some help in pulling the dead body of that women outside the pond, but he was not in a condition to understand or even realise what happened. I then entered the pond. My first step touched something fluffy underneath the water surface. Instantly, another dead body emerged out from under the water. I was frightened and immediately came out of the water, huffing in massive distress. My breath became irregular too. I could not understand what was going on.

Moments later, I saw hundreds of corpses emerging out and floating in the pond. Bodies were twice their actual size due to inflammation. I recognised a few of them. Those who prepared themselves to fight for their freedom got freed from their lives forever. That scene haunted me so much so that I fell to the ground almost unconscious. It was evident to me that bandits attacked after I left for the cemetery. After remaining inactive on the field for some time, I suddenly jumped into the pond and began inspecting each dead body. Making my way through ginormous piles of corpses I searched every single one of them. I looked for Tara's body in that pond but could not find her.

I came out of the pond and ran towards the neighbourhood so that I could search for Tara in each house. Halfway through my way to the neighbourhood, something stopped me suddenly. It was my mind compelling me to check that area again. Before I could go and check the houses, I turned around and decided to check into the well that was built nearby the pond. My steps took so long to cover the same distance I covered in seconds initially. Probably, the fear of finding Tara dead was killing me. The closer I came to the well, shakier my legs became. I sweated profusely and shivered with cold. With all the courage left in me, I peeped into the well and instantly took few steps back in distress. Tara was inside the well, lying almost naked with her eyes wide open. I could not cry anymore, and I stood there still for a while. Without any reaction, I proceeded towards the well with an intention to end my life right there, right then. There was so much of annihilation, so much of darkness all over that I, for the first time in my life feared death. I could not jump into the well and ran back to that deranged man I saw while entering the village.

"How did you not die with them? Why did they leave you untouched! Why??" I squeezed his throat with both hands and asked him brutally.

"I swear on God I will kill you now, answer me! Why are you the only one who is alive here? You are one of them, aren't you!!" I, influenced by my anger almost suffocated him.

"They saw this royal stamp on my wrist and knew I was not among the villagers. They knew I was sent here by the king for some reason. They did not want to do anything that could put them under the king's fury. The killing of royal personnel is deemed as initiating an act of war against the kingdom. That is why I am alive," he answered.

"Why did the king send you here?" I asked further.

"I am a spy. He saw you and Tara one day in the field while you trained these villagers. He sent me here to keep an eye on you both," he confessed.

"The night you left brought bad omen to this village. Bandits attacked a few hours after your departure. The sun had not risen yet. But many of the villagers left their house. Thieves made an announcement for the villagers to surrender everything to them. Nobody came out this time. Bandits became furious, and they forcefully pulled one family out of their house. Seeing their torture on that family, few people, mostly women and elderly came out to their rescue. They too were attacked by the bandits. Suddenly, whoever was present in the neighbourhood at that time came out with whatever they had with them to use as a weapon. Bandits didn't expect that type of retaliation. They could not think of anything but to attack and protect themselves from the villagers. A fierce battle took place.

Men, women, elders and children all fought like warriors. They were not letting it go. Some grabbed few of the bandits and pulled them on the ground from their horses. It was then when one of them discharged a flare in the sky and moments later many more bandits came with massive arms and artillery. Those people fought bravely but could not outnumber the villains. That pond does not only have villagers in it... it is filled with many of those bastards as well! Tara fought bravely. She singlehandedly took many of them down. You said it right that she had got warrior's blood running through her veins. I could not see that gruesome ghastly battle, so I ran away someplace safe. And now you found her in the well, all tired and serene. She happily sacrificed her life protecting others. You should not have gone Eklavya! You should have stayed!" he further explained to me. I was in tears. The volcano of my emotions erupted with a loud scream.

"She asked me if she could come with me to the cemetery. She wanted me to be safe all the time... I did not let her go with me. I should have. I did wrong to her! I am their culprit... It is me who let them die. It is me who let her die! I should not have trained them in first place... It is all my fault... Tara! Please forgive me! Forgive me for my sins... I killed those innocent people. What have I done?? Oh! Lord, what have I done?" I repented and remained sitting helplessly beside the man.

Figure: The lost legion - Corpses of the villagers floating in the pond.

23: Tragic Separation

EKLAVYA

It was late in the night, and I along with that royal spy laid on the ground. As it was a new moon night couple of days ago, the moon was barely visible in the sky. Stars were, however, compensating for its dim light as they collectively emitted more amount of light than the moon could. Straightaway, I heard some neighing of horses from far away and immediately got up and sat, looking abruptly in the direction where the sound was coming from. I pushed the spy that was lying almost dead. I heard the neighing mixed with the distant crisp thumping sound of horses' steps.

"Bandits are here! They are here again, they are in search of any living being here, they will kill us now... Hide quickly!!" frightened man stood up and ran into one of the houses, locking the door from inside. Until a few seconds ago, he did not even show any signs of life except for breathing and now the fear of death induced a charge in his body that made him run like a cheetah. I disgraced his cowardice. I could not walk and so, remained seated silently. Waiting for those horses to come from inside the vegetation nearby, I looked up at the sky and wondered if Maa and Father saw all that from above. I wondered if all dead people really become stars. At a younger age, I listened to the stories of *Amma* that made me believe that all good souls become stars and watch their loved ones from the above. Friction on the ground became intense, and bushes and plants revealed some horsemen coming from inside them. Darkness made it hard to see small things and details from a distance. I saw them as they were many in number, but I was not sure if they had seen me sitting there. I was tired living my life, giving up on it after losing Tara and everyone else to that catastrophic Armageddon.

Those horsemen searched for any living individuals in the village. I debated if that spy was right. All those riders knew what they were doing. They had a synchronisation among them, they were not in a hurry and behaved like a professional search and rescue team. Also, they had some extra horses apparently with some first aid materials loaded on their backs. I understood that those men on horses were king's regiment and not bandits and thought of calling that spy back so that he could meet with his people and go back to the kingdom safely but then I waited to be sure about my guess.

"Did you find anyone there??" one of them shouted.

"Captain! I found many in the pond... but all dead!" replied the other soldier with a sharp voice.

"Keep searching... there has to be at least someone alive! Look carefully for our man among the dead," the captain commanded.

Now it was clear to me that those men were the royal army and not bandits.

"I found some more corpses in the well, Captain!" shouted another soldier.

"We have to take everybody out of the water!" captain commanded, and all the soldiers began pulling out the bodies from the water. They had fought so many battles and saw so many deaths in their career in the regiment. But that massacre in the village was something unimaginable that put each one of them in severe despondency, and they all began losing their courage.

"We did not have to witness this disaster if the king would have stepped up against those dacoits... What a loser he is!" the captain expressed his agony.

"If only he gave up on those state-sponsored amusements and worked for the betterment of the people of his state..." said another one in sorrow.

They pulled every dead body out of the pond and that well in a very little time. The soldiers became silent in tremendous grief upon looking at so many self-destroyed dead bodies at once. There was a stinking smell in the air too.

"Let's go! I do not think there is any survivor left here. It seems our man also got killed. We shall come back in few hours and scrutinise each one of them under the sun," the captain said.

"Let's go tell the king about the possible demise of our spy and these innocent people of this small slum," he further said to all the soldiers, and they slowly began retreating.

"Your man is inside that house, hiding from you all and in the fear that you would kill him," I spoke loudly, and they all stopped and looked at me sitting on the ground with my head bent down. Few of them ran towards me. Perhaps, they all were surprised and happy to see someone alive in that barren land of corpses. I kept my finger pointing at the house in which that spy hid from those soldiers. Few of them rushed to get him out of the house.

"Who are you? Are you alright?" asked the captain.

"I am Eklavya, a stranger to this village! My friend brought me here, and she is dead now," I replied with my pride of being an Ikshvaku shaken. My lineage gave nothing to me, it was only karma and kismet that performed their art on the canvas of my life. Even before the captain could ask some more questions, those soldiers brought the spy out of the house. He was still under the trauma but recognised his men and at the same time was afraid of them. He had his conscious intact, yet he acted weird, he was happy to see them and at the same time was in distress. His condition was strange and unknown to others. Everybody knew that he suffered from devastating trauma.

"Are there any more survivors?" the captain asked.

"No! Nobody is here! They all are dead... I am their culprit... I killed them!! You just pulled Tara out of the well... I killed her... I am her killer!! Kill me now... I don't want to live anymore!" I could not control my emotions and lost my senses again.

"Take him too with us! I don't want to lose him as he could be the source of some vital information to the king.", the captain ordered his soldiers.

"But we have our man to tell everything that took place here," suggested one of them.

"He is almost dead, mentally! And dead men tell no tales! We are taking this boy with us!" the captain justified his decision.

"No, leave me! Don't touch me... I am not going anywhere without Tara...Tara!! Tara!!" I shouted, but soldiers tightly grabbed my arm, taking me towards their horses. They made the spy sit on one of the extra horses they had brought, and one soldier sat on another horse with me seated in the front. Captain kicked his horse, and it trotted. All others followed. My scream gradually went distant from Tara as I was being taken away from her.

"If my desperate want of winning over him were visible, the air would have been crimson that morning."

- Pundir (*Long Live the Sullied*)

24: Royal Confrontation

TIME

Outside the royal palace, the sun spread its golden shade in the sky. Birds in the capital region of Rudraputra chirped in subtle decorum. As if they knew they lived in the king's palace and maintaining their difference from 'other' birds was important. People were blessed with all the luxury and well-being universe could give to them. There were no beggars, no helpless, no friction between people, no commotion and no commoners to be seen near the palace. It was all superficial to Eklavya.

'How can such fame and glory be in the capital of a corrupt king? Certainly, there is somebody doing something good in his court except the king, the king must have some wise and noble souls in his cabinet,' wondered Eklavya while standing behind the bars of one of the armoured cabins built outside the palace. He was kept in the captivity with such arrangements that made him believe as if he was some sort of highly wanted criminal of all times. Pondering upon the novice actions of the soldiers last night he caught the impression of the birds flying freely in the sky and felt a tinge of jealousy in his heart for their liberation and freedom. While he was restless in captivity, he knew that the king will ask for his presence on the court soon. He was still shaken from inside but prepared to confront with the king of Rudraputra for the first time.

Inside the royal palace, on the other hand, all the security personnel, cooks, gardeners, kitchen staff, cleaning staff and everyone else got up and got busy in their own work. The cabinet of ministers under the supervision of *Maha-Mantri*, was already in the court discussing the arrangement of the governance in outskirts of the region. General population who wanted to see the trials attended the royal court in those days. People from various villages and towns were present in the court that day as that was no ordinary day on the court. The day held remarkable importance as Eklavya, and that spy had to appear in the court before the king.

There was a lot of fuss going on in the court. Ministers and people discussed with each other about their opinion of what was going to happen with Eklavya and the spy. It was brought to the attention of the cabinet of ministers that some lucky survivors of the last night's catastrophe had come to seek help, protection and refuge in the palace. The court eagerly waited for the arrival of the king. The people of the state and the staff inside the palace would wake up in the morning and get busy in their own work, whereas, the king would often wake up late in the morning. To him, the value and significance of the royal responsibility and the crown that was passed onto him in patrimonial heritage was nothing more than the source of pleasure and meant for resting in its luxury. He always did what his cabinet suggested him to do. He had no sense of leadership and judgement left in him anymore. There had been times when he rejected the wise decision of the cabinet and did almost opposite of what was suggested, just to prove his supremacy over them and everyone else in the state. And who could have stopped him from doing that? After all, he was the king of Rudraputra. He was weak from his body, dull from his wisdom, corrupt from the character and he always thought of his happiness alone. His daily routine included hunting animals for pleasure, spending money and resources on unnecessary things like organising *mujra* performed by courtesans and spending time in brothels.

The morning converted itself into noon and Eklavya was still captured inside the cabin. He became restless and frustrated with the kind of treatment he got. After realising he could not do much about his situation he sat quietly inside the metallic cube. A soldier flicked a plate full of meal towards him from under the bottom of the bars. He was hungry, but in anger, he slid the food back to the soldier. The soldier took the food back without saying anything to him. Eklavya then realised his foolishness, wishing he would have just taken the food.

Soon afterwards the king came to the court. Most of the mass was already standing while those who were sitting, stood in his honour and the king sat down on his throne, which was made a little bigger and higher than everybody else's chair. Once the king settled down, all ministers sat down too. After discussing some minor issues and telling jokes to each other, *Maha-Mantri* told the king about the attack on the village near the hill last night. The king listened to some formally explained facts and instances and vaguely expressed his concern and anxiety.

The king did all that to make and maintain a safe and trustworthy image of him to the public. He had to win the confidence of his people to peacefully reap the benefits of the crown.

Soon it was brought to his notice that some people escaped that massacre and were willing to seek kingdom's protection and refuge in the capital. The king also came to know that his spy was alive. He ordered his ministers to present the spy and Eklavya into the court. The eagerness of the people increased, the discussion began to rise once more among them. Eklavya saw some soldiers coming towards him, and he understood that he will be taken to court. He stood up while preparing himself mentally for that big moment. The soldiers put the chains in his hands and started taking him with them. Upon reaching outside the palace, Eklavya forgot the pain he was experiencing before due to the heavy chains tied to his hands and body. 'Those who stay here in this beautiful palace are more fortunate than those who live in the villages,' he thought.

EKLAVYA

I entered the palace and felt a cold breeze on my face with a sweet fragrance of jasmine flowers. The palace illuminated with lights emitting from fancy candles and lanterns that put the sunlight to the shame. The doorway of the court inside the castle was bigger than the field in which I trained the villagers for the battle. Upon being taken near the door, two guards opened the door of the court. I saw hundreds of people sitting in big chairs. Glitter in their golden dresses and jewellery mesmerised me for some time, or maybe more, I don't know. I was lost in the sumptuous richness of the court filled with people, decorated with big glass windows with silk curtains hanging on them, velvety smooth carpets and huge golden statues and idols of Hindu Gods and Goddesses. It was then when a soldier pulled me with the chain ahead, and I realised that I was brought as a captive there and not as a guest to the royal family. The King's throne was straight ahead in front of the entry gate. I could not notice it as I was looking here and there agape in fascination. Moreover, hundreds of unknown eyes looked at me all at once, which made me conscious of my appearance. I was simply stunned to see the court's great infrastructure and lavish interior. Someone like me who spent his childhood in a small village, adulthood in the cemetery and suffered for a few days in the jungle fighting for his survival would never even dream of that palace ever.

Meanwhile, soldiers left me in front of the king. I looked straight into his eyes. I was a little frustrated, angry and worried about what was going to happen to me next. As I appeared to be an ordinary boy to the king, he ordered the guards to remove the chains from my body. I also saw that spy standing still right beside me. Even before I could talk to him...

"What have you seen during those five days spent in the village?" the king asked the spy.

"After you left for hunting the other day, I joined those people in their training in the field. Eklavya and his friend Tara taught fighting skills to the villagers. People religiously honed their skills as they wanted to eliminate the threat of hill bandits forever.

Yesterday even before the sunrise, bandits attacked the village. Those who could fight with them fought bravely. Nobody surrendered to the bandits this time. Some grabbed the bandits and killed them ruthlessly. It was then when bandits called for help, and in minutes many of them arrived in the village. A fierce battle took place but bandits being more in number and with heavy arms killed all the people. Not being able to separate the dead bodies of their people from those of the villagers, they threw all of them in the pond in frustration and distress. Some of the villagers jumped into the well to protect themselves but drowned. However, this boy was not there in the fight. He was gone from the village one night before the attack. Something did not seem right to me, Lord! That is all I had to say," he told the king and was ordered to retreat.

"This boy is the reason for our losses! He tricked us into his brainwashing skills and provoked us to fight with the bandits... He purposely vanished somewhere leaving us strangled to fight and to be killed... He should be punished for his misleading deeds! He should be hanged!!... He is the reason for that battle. Kill him! Kill him!" those who escaped the battle and were seeking refuge shouted and demanded my death. They blamed me for that catastrophe, showing their coward self. I could not believe my ears, and stood there in shock, wondering about the hypocrite behaviour of those remaining people from the village. 'These hypocrites should not have been spared!

Why they did not get killed in the battle?!' I cursed them in my mind, soon realising my vice and pondered upon what *Kali*, the evil did to my thinking. I regretted the cursing thought and moved on inside my mind.

Ministers told those people to keep calm and stand quietly. Ministers were wise, and they knew merely shouting, and frustration of those victims would not prove me to be guilty of that incident.

"Do you want to say something in your defence?" one of them asked me.

"Why there is no seating arrangement for the commoners in this royal court? How can you mount on these glittering high seats while watching fellow people standing for an extended period? And I see all men here, why there is no woman in the cabinet??" I questioned the minister while looking at the king as I was keeping myself from asking that question since I entered the court. There was an awkward silence in the courtroom for a second. Seemed as if some people simply did not understand what I just said. Perhaps they were surprised to see me asking questions that were tough to ask and even tougher to answer in that court Instead of defending myself. The ministers looked amazed; the king was stunned!

"Don't try to deviate us from the issue! There has been a charge put upon you of conspiring a mass murder. Don't you have anything to say in your defence? You could be hanged; don't you fear your death??" asked another minister.

"Ha ha! Death is nothing to worry about. What haunts me is living a life with hypocrite people like these standing in your courtroom!" I said, pointing towards those villagers who just had blamed me for everything happened in the recent past. I was confident and replied with a bold voice, reflecting my fearless attitude towards life.

"Even if I explain everything before this court, no one is going to believe me. All I can say is I did not spend so many days teaching them how to combat just to see them die. I did not leave my friend, my saviour, Tara with them to die an unfair death! I could have taken her with me. Moreover, I would have never come back into the village had I been involved in any manner in this unfortunate event!! And most importantly, I would not have stayed and wailed all night long in that deserted village with your spy just to get myself captured by your men!" I further explained. The king along with the ministers and everyone else thought about my justification that seemed to be convincing.

"Who are you?" asked the king.

"I am Eklavya. The son of Vyas and the scion of Ikshvaku," I said with my head held high and with restored pride.

"I was born in a small village situated on the banks of the Ganges in the north of your state. I lost my mother, father and *Amma*. My people abandoned me and forced me to leave my village forever. It was then when I was brought into the cemetery situated in the south of the Ganges. I grew up there under the care of the old man who nurtured me like my family would have done. Then something happened, and I found the brutal answers and reasons for all my misfortunate events happened in my life when I was younger. I decided to leave the cemetery for an undetermined period. I was stuck in the jungle and was captured by the tribal people. They thought I was sent by you to intrude them and to leak their secrets so that Rudraputra can attack their tribe and expand its boundaries in the jungle too. Somehow Tara rescued me and brought me to the village near the hill. I then got to know that bandits often robbed and tortured these villagers. I also got to know that villagers brought this issue into your notice several times in the past, but you always turned a blind eye to their requests. You fell deeply into the materialistic pleasures of your kingdom. I then decided to teach them how to fight for their lives. What wrong did I do in that? It was my dharma to prevent their lives and belongings from being taken away by those hooligans, and I just did so.

One night before the attack, I got the news that the caretaker of the cemetery was seeking my presence in his last days. I had to go visit him anyhow. He was like a father to me! I told Tara to take care of these villagers. When I came back, I saw your spy sitting in deep remorse under a tree in the village. I didn't see anybody else and asked him the reason why nobody was there in the village. He told me about the attack, and I could not believe what destiny had done to us. During all these years, I faced so many enemies, so much hatred, immense pain and saw plenty of deaths that I do not fear my death now! I am not afraid to die. But I am afraid to live with those who don't have their character and morale intact. I am afraid to live in oblivion. I am afraid of being cheated by my life and destiny!" I was done talking, and tears rolled down my eyes.

"Nice story that was!" the king exclaimed while all the ministers regretted upon his naïve sense of understanding.

"Take this criminal away and put him in the jail until I decide for his punishment." he ordered, and few guards stood to capture me again as per the royal decree.

"I testify what this boy just said, my Lord! I know he would never conspire against anyone. I confirm his identity!" a loud and clear voice emerged, and guards stopped coming towards me for a moment as the person who spoke was of high rank and dignity in the court.

"What are you saying *Maha-Mantri*?" the king was surprised after listening to that. I looked at the person who said so, shaking my head and blinking my eyes several times to make myself believe what I just saw.

'*Maha-Purohit*! *Maha-Purohit*!!' my mind brawled with shock. The *Maha-Mantri* of the kingdom was none other than the *Maha-Purohit* himself. He was almost unrecognisable in the royal dress and with a sword hung around his waist. There was a charm in his eyes and good faith in his voice.

All the ministers looked at each other without any clue. People murmured among themselves again, and the king could not understand what was going on there.

"I knew his father very well. I knew his mother very well. He comes from a very reputed family, my Lord! Eklavya would never do such misleading and horrendous deeds in his life. I had been to the cemetery he was talking about. Also, I had met the old man whom he had lived with for many years. He is telling the truth! I testify his claims. He is innocent," *Maha-Mantri* further clarified.

"It is against the law to punish someone innocent. What happened was just an unfortunate course of the fate that Eklavya had no control over. Punishing him will betray the trust of the people in law and order in this kingdom. He is harmless and absolutely not guilty of anything," he finished talking and sat down.

"*Maha-Mantri* said it right, Eklavya must not get any punitive punishment or any punishment for that matter for something he had not done," ministers constituted their consensus on the same. Apparently, the king was left with no other option but to order my release. He could still do anything except giving me a death sentence but luckily decided to just set me free.

"*Maha-Mantri*! It is your responsibility to keep an eye on him. You take this boy under your supervision and include him in our army. He can be an asset to us. If he can teach those weak and innocent villagers how to fight, he can teach something to our brave and fearless soldiers too! Give shelter to these victims as well!" the king gave his verdict and left immediately for his amusement in the brothel.

There was a commotion in the courtroom. People retreated towards their homes, ministers congratulated *Maha-Mantri* upon influencing the king and stopping him from giving one more unjust verdict.

And I stood still and stunned, looking at *Maha-Purohit* and making my mind believe if he was the same person whom I had known since my birth. I was astounded to see him and could not believe it was the same person who was repenting in grief and asking for my forgiveness for the sins he had committed in the past. I could not believe that it was the same man whom I was giving wisdom and direction to do some good to others in the remaining days of his life. It was the same *Maha-Purohit* who hated my family so much so that he killed them for gaining higher influence on others. The same person had saved me from being hanged today, he had protected the righteous, the same person had just shown an exemplary example of holding more wisdom than he had before, the same person just influenced the king who happened to be the most powerful man in Rudraputra. The same person indeed was not the same anymore!

25: Transition of Belief

MAHA-PUROHIT

The night was about to prevail, and most of the staff members in the palace prepared for their sleep. Night guards and maintenance personnel inside the palace began their shift. Eklavya and I had just left the royal kitchen after eating dinner. We had to walk through a hallway to get to the other side of the palace. Eklavya still struggled to understand that remarkable upside down change he saw in me, and I still regretted whatever I did to him in the past. Thus, we both had not talked to each other yet.

"As per the order of the king, you will stay with me. There is enough space for two people in the room," I told him after accumulating some courage. Finally, the awkward silence of guilt and stress broke.

"How did you reach here? And why do they recognise you as their *Maha-Mantri* and not *Maha-Purohit*?" he asked eagerly and was not at all worried about where he was going to stay or with whom.

"Sshh! Talk low, walls do have ears here! Let's get into the room and then I will tell you everything," I said anxiously. We went in, and I shut the door immediately. Eklavya gave me a thoughtful gaze.

"Your harsh but true words that day killed all the evil in my heart. I went in sheer remorse and in search of redemption decided that the atonement of my sins will surely be done before I die. Since then I have always put whatever humane had left inside me for the good of the others. What demonic deed I had done can't be undone! But indeed, I can do my bit to compensate for the harm I caused to others. That day after being told to leave the cemetery, my ego was shattered! I was not the same person anymore. I had to bring everything back on track... Everything that I could bring back to normal.

While retreating to a location then unknown, I realised that the system can't be changed by staying out of the system. I would have to become a part of the system to alter it effectively. So, I headed straight to the capital from the cemetery. I was already celebrated as Rudraputra's *Maha-Purohit* and had served the Kingdom's capital for past so many years with rites & rituals, royal ceremonies and astrological predictions. The king's family knew my father, and he came to see me after knowing that I was in the capital that day. He expressed his concern about the ministers and staff leaving the palace in vengeance. Vengeance for his manhandled way of ruling Rudraputra. Nobody wanted to work for him. He was failing big time as a ruler.

Upon asking me for the solution to this problem I told him it was not going to be solved by some astrological gimmick. Rather, he should ponder upon the way of administering the state. The king was submerged in the oblivion. He could not think beyond the virtue of worldly pleasures and offered me to join his court as *Maha-Mantri*, hoping I would prove to be a great help in telling him what to do and how to maintain the rule of law in Rudraputra. He was right! I would now help him build a better state, helping him differently though. Seemed like the almighty himself gave that opportunity to me to enter the system and change it for the greater good. I could not deny and accepted the offer only on one condition that no interference shall be created in my way of working. Without thinking much about his decision, he agreed, and on the same day I was officially assigned with the designation," I explained everything to Eklavya.

"That is why those guards stopped after you stepped in for my defence in the court!" he exclaimed.

"Yes! They had to stop," I replied.

"Destiny had planned something greater for you, son! By the astounding wills of the fate, you arrived here. And now that you are here, you must play your part in the redemption of the Kingdom. You will play your role in the biggest reform of the power in Rudraputra," I further continued.

"I am debating whether I should try to do something courageous or not. Every time I tried to resolve things in the past, I was backlashed with tremendous force by the universe. It all seems like planned episodes of tyranny. When I look back in time, I see a painful life! I see no hope; will I ever see hope in the future? A hopeful time for myself and for the people of my clan and for all of the humanity," he asked me with a saddened voice.

"With each passing hour, the darkness of the night becomes persistent. Darkness prevails but only to ensure that the hope is near. The hope, the morning and the light are near, Eklavya!" I somehow tried to enlighten the already awakened one.

"What is that you want me to play a role in? How can I help you, myself and the people of Rudraputra? How can I fulfil my father's dream of a peaceful world? If I could be any help for the betterment of the state, tell me! I seek a purpose, I would even die for it! I have taken such course that no man had taken first, dreamt of becoming the source of change, the dream that my father had dreamed once," he was confident and all set to participate in the reform.

"I know you are not afraid to die. You don't have to die, son! Death does not want to take on with you anytime soon. Those who must die will die for sure. Time will come when you will be included in the plan. It's late night now, get some sleep. You have to meet our soldiers and other staff in the morning," I dimmed the flame of the lantern and laid in my bed.

He went in the bed perhaps wondering about what I had said about the plan. Admiring the moonlight tryst from one of the windows in the room I pondered upon what the next morning would bring for us. Soon, I gave myself into the world of dreams.

26: The Secret Meeting

EKLAVYA

It was a little late than midnight, and the palace was devoid of any motion inside it. Night guards guarded the main gate as the garrison of the palace. I took a turn in the bed and with semi-conscious sight, noticed *Maha-Purohit* was not in his bed. I could not listen to any sound from inside the room too. My eyes opened utterly in surprise.

'Where could he possibly go at this time of the night and why would he?' I thought and waited for some time in the bed. He did not return till then, and I soon fell asleep again. The next day I was awakened by him from my sleep.

"Since, when did you begin to sleep till this late? The old man had better control over your laziness for you would wake up early in the morning in the cemetery," he commented.

"I haven't slept properly in months! This was perhaps the most serene and peaceful night I had ever spent lately," I justified.

"You and the king have this similar habit of getting up late… Who knows one day you might get the kingship of Rudraputra," he toyed with the idea, and I looked at him in sheer pessimism.

"Get ready quickly! We are going to see our people and meet with our troops," he ordered and walked out of the room. I left the bed immediately and went for a shower, missing plunging into the Ganges for bathing when I lived in the cemetery. Meanwhile, *Maha-Purohit* arranged for a uniform for me and also took the consent of the king for giving me the right to wear the uniform and to access the sensitive areas of the kingdom. The king had an unshakable trust in *Maha-Mantri*'s way of managing things. Without any due, he told *Maha-Mantri* to include me into the army.

The royal wagon was arranged for us to visit the cantonment. The cart reminded me of the chariot *Gurukul* used to have. The only difference was in the number of horses. *Gurukul*'s chariot had two horses while the royal one had only one. It requires more power to climb up the hill, that's why. *Maha-Purohit* and I sat in the wagon. The driver held the reins tightly and gave his horse some slack. The horse fluttered his long ears back and swiftly picked up its pace.

"The atmosphere of the capital is very different from your village and cemetery. We all lived like a big family in villages. We all worked as a cohort there. But this capital region of Rudraputra is filled with those who are bound to think for themselves only. Taxes are high, the education system is shattered, agricultural land is decreasing, medical facilities are going down, and internal peace is going away from the state. In their own country, they live like nomads.

Look! Those children are supposed to go to the *Gurukul*. Instead, they are helping their parents in the field. They could not afford to educate their children. How serious would their condition be? Almost everything from their earning goes into the king's pocket. Besides, see the land on which they are performing agriculture. Even if they fully utilise the land, it is so small to feed them for the next few months, leave alone feeding the entire community. Civic facilities are so expensive that ordinary man can't even think of affording it. King has put almost everything in expanding the army and ammunition. What would the army do if there is no peace and well-being inside the state? What are we protecting from our enemies? Poorness? Devastation? Or just the area of this land in distress? These people are good at heart, they are just in trouble," sitting inside the horse-wagon, *Maha-Purohit* brought my attention to some of the severe conditions in the capital. I was in pain, looking agape at the ruined world all around me.

"If Rudraputra does not get any efficient ruler soon, it will witness a rebellion. Most of the army and civilians will declare war against their king. There will be a catastrophic uprising. We have to do something about it!" he muttered in worry.

"I will try to convince the army men of your headship of the army. If they agree, then there is no way the king would object. Just don't react to my statements in front of them. I will have to play some mind games for the greater good. Trust me, my intentions will be pure in future," he suggested while I couldn't get my head around what I just heard.

"The cantonment is here, *Maha-Mantri*!" the wagon driver informed.

"Stay here until we come back," he said to the charioteer who nodded in affirmative, and we proceeded inside the cantonment. As everyone in the cantonment saw their *Maha-Mantri*, they all gathered around. Some saluted him, some greeted him while others brought chairs and water for us.

"He is Eklavya! Our new member of the army," he briefly introduced me to the rest of the troop.

"Brave-hearts! Fearless sentinels of the state!! I came here today to inform you about a significant change in the administration. I know most of you all were the citizens of this state even before this young boy was born. You all have devoted everything for the protection of Rudraputra. Many of us sacrificed their lives for the motherland. Despite being in dire need of resources, you all put in whatever you had just to ensure the safety of the people. So, it might not be easy for many of you to abide by the orders from someone who might seem naïve at first! As per the royal orders, Eklavya, with immediate effect, is the in charge of the army of Rudraputra."

Maha-Mantri was cut in between by the commotion that arose after listening to his declaration.

"How can that be possible? One must serve in the army before becoming eligible for the post of in charge," said someone in the crowd.

"I know the law! But there is a provision of overriding the general rule especially if the king himself demands so. Didn't you know that?!" he muffled everybody's doubts.

"What is the proof that this boy has skills and aptitude at least at par with us?" asked another soldier. *Maha-Mantri* continued,

"I don't have to show you any evidence..." and he was interrupted by a bold voice from behind.

"I am Eklavya! Scion of Ikshvaku and your commander. I am ready to show my skills and aptitude in front of this gathering. I don't want any responsibility on my shoulders that deem unfair to you all. Tell me what I should show you to prove my eligibility to become an army in charge?" I spoke with my chest filled with pride.

"Anyone up for one to one fight with Eklavya?" *Maha-Mantri* asked in confidence.

"Bheema...Bheema!! Bheema!!" crowd cheered for their mighty warrior, Bheema.

A large man from the crowd came out and bowed to *Maha-Mantri*. I got amazed at the very sight of Bheema. *Maha-Mantri* was already aware how humungous Bheema was.

"Are you sure you want to do this? There is still time to stop this," he asked me for the final approval.

"Come what may in the way, the son of Ikshvaku must not retreat in apprehension! I am ready!!" I replied and had already started planning in my mind upon how to defeat Bheema, applying all special moves that *Acharya* Virbhadra taught me. I had won over the man inside my mind. Now, all I had to do was just to win over Bheema in reality.

Seeing a bad match between both the fighters *Maha-Mantri* thought of giving some weapon to us. That per him would help me in winning. So, he immediately brought two wooden swords and handed us each. A circle was made in the middle of the gathering for the fight. Bheema and I bowed to each other with respect and honour. The match started after *Maha-Mantri* commanded us to begin. I remembered Tara fighting the bear and stood, in the same way, holding the sword. The crowd looked surprised to see the attitude of a young adult boy fighting with an experienced and mighty warrior.

Fierce attacks emerged from both sides. Bheema's powerful slashes haunted the spectators. I, on the other hand, focused on swiftness and easily dodged his attacks. I would not want to come inside his attacking range. As Bheema was huge, he began losing his breath soon. I, no matter how fast I was, took some thrusts on my body and screamed in immense pain. But I was not ready to let it go. I knew he will be out of stamina soon. After some time, I got an opportunity to attack his leg. Bheema now stood in the middle of the circle, unable to move his big structure around the arena. The crowd could anticipate the result, *Maha-Mantri* calmed down as I finished the fight by pointing the edge of the sword on his head. All it took was just a few minutes to end the fight. All of them were pleased to see my fighting skills and determination. We hugged each other in appreciation and Bheema embraced my victory. Everyone seemed to develop confidence in me as their in-charge. After discussing some future plans with the soldiers *Maha-Mantri* and I left for the palace.

"What happened to him?" the charioteer asked with surprise and concern.

"He had a friendly introduction with Bheema!" *Maha-Mantri* replied. We all laughed, and wagon headed to the palace.

Upon reaching the palace, everyone there asked about my condition. *Maha-Mantri* had to explain everything to everybody. The king too got to know about my victory over Bheema and gained confidence in my capabilities. The court was filled with mixed reactions. Some appreciated the idea of me becoming the in-charge while some criticised the insensitive decision of the king. But they all were impressed by my actions. After having dinner in the royal kitchen, *Maha-Purohit* and I headed towards our room. It became hard for the sun to prevail over the darkness. The night sky glimmered with billions of the stars shining like silver dots. *Maha-Purohit* redressed my bandages and dimmed the lantern. We both went to bed, but I could not sleep that night. Partially because of the pain in wounds I had got in the fight and rest because I wanted to see if he would go out of his room that night or not. After a little later than midnight, I heard some squeak from the other bed. Seemed as if he got up from the bed. I was all ears and listened to the opening of the door of the room and then closing too. I forgot about my pain for some time. I also left the bed in a snap and followed him quietly. I was thrilled and excited at the same time. 'Now what evil he is planning for?' I thought while secretly following him in the hallway. *Maha-Purohit* went to a direction unexplored by me yet. I did not hesitate to go there and kept on following him. Soon, he exited via a secret window into the wild and so did I. He was well aware of the palace and knew that there were no night guards in that area of the building where he just passed from.

I hid in the bushes, slightly far away from where he stood. Seemed as if he was waiting for someone to join him. 'Who else comes here in the wilderness and ghostly night to meet *Maha-Purohit*?' I wondered in tremendous thrill. I waited and waited in the bushes for that someone who was expected to meet with him that night but did not see anyone coming. I also feared being caught by the guards or *Maha-Purohit* and was about to return to the palace. Instantly, I saw some yellow points of lights coming towards where he stood.

'Oh, Lord! What is this man up to?' I felt a shivering sensation in my body. Those dots of lights were lanterns in the hands of some people disguised inside their blankets. Soon, I saw some of the army men, all the ministers of the royal court and few other unrecognised people gathering around *Maha-Purohit*. My mind was full of presumptions as I was utterly curious to discover that secret meeting. I tried to listen to their conversation but was unable to catch up anything apparently.

'Kingdom, tomorrow, why, he... Coup (inaudible), Eklavya, kill evil,' that is what I could barely hear and could not understand anything. After sensing the end of the meeting slightly ahead of time, I retreated towards my room via the same path and through the same secret window. For a moment, I thought I forgot the right way of returning to the room, but luckily, I made it and quickly went to bed. Soon after, the door opened and closed. *Maha-Purohit* entered and lay on his bed silently, but I was wide awake and didn't sleep that night.

He was surprised to see me sitting in my bed even before the sunrise the next morning. After seeing my eyes red and mind immersed in deep thinking he asked me if everything was alright. I nodded in affirmative and at the same time debated as to when I should confront him about those meetings in the nights. I decided to give some time to my notions and got ready for the training. That day, I formed different groups of the soldiers who had similar expertise and liking for certain weapons. Just as I did with those villagers. Some liked to fight with swords, some with spears, some had maces while others preferred nothing but their fists and kicks. I saw some of the men in the regiment who were present at the last night's meeting. They all acted perfectly normal with each other and with *Maha-Mantri.* As if nothing was of grave concern for them and those meetings were just their regular routine followed at a weird time. Something of utmost significance was about to occur for sure, and I badly wanted to know what it was all about before it would be too late to do anything about that.

The day went well, and I returned to the palace with *Maha-Purohit.* I asked him if I could meet with some active learners among the troops before leaving for the castle. He gave me the permission. I chose all those men whom I saw last night in the meeting. Nobody could smell that I knew about their secret gatherings. I wanted to learn more about those people and discovered that those men were previously elected as high ranked officials until the king dismissed them from their ranks for some stupid reasons and appointed his loyal but incapable men in the army. Things made some better sense in my mind.

I came back to the palace along with *Maha-Purohit* and had dinner with the rest of the staff in the royal kitchen. It was time for us to rest. I had already decided to catch them all red-handed that night, eagerly waiting for *Maha-Purohit* to leave for the meeting. Because of being awake since past day and profoundly exhausted, I never knew when I fell asleep. When I opened my eyes, he was gone already. Without waiting for a second, I too left the room and quickly reached the bushes and stood in a concealed point. As soon as they all gathered I prepared myself for how I was going to approach them. I was unaware of their intentions and had a fear of being attacked by those men.

"Do not move! It's me, Eklavya!" I shouted and ran towards them. They all feared my sudden and loud scream. However, me catching them red-handed did not bother them at all.

"How did you reach here? What are you doing here!?" *Maha-Purohit* asked me with a disturbed voice.

"I ask you the same question, what are you all doing here in the night? I have been watching you gather here for the past few days… what's going on here? Why are you not keeping me in the loop? Am I not your army-in-charge??" I asked.

"We were deciding on the right time to bring you into the plan. Remember, I told you that you must play your role in bringing everything back on the right track?" *Maha-Purohit* reminded me.

"Yes. And I said I would even die for the greater good of the people and Rudraputra. But what is the plan?" I am sure I had an innocent expression on my face at that moment. Few lanterns had run out of the fuel and remaining barely gave enough light to see anything. They all decided to tell me about their plan in the morning. Nobody wanted to create chaos in the night that would ruin their plan even before it's conceived.

"I am amazed by your stealth skills!" *Maha-Purohit* said while returning to the palace.

"And I am worried about your hidden motives!" I expressed my frustration.

"You shall not worry about that. What is worth worrying has not been disclosed to you yet," he told me, and I surrendered myself to the night. I am not sure if *Maha-Purohit* went to sleep after that, for that eunuch might have some more secret things going on, who knows?

27: The Coup

EKLAVYA

I was told to come to the court next day as the king had to collect the taxes from the commoners and ministers wanted me to see that. Upon reaching there, I found huge lineups of helpless people having their hard-earned money in their hands. There was no arrangement for their seating as they all stood under the summer sun. Children, elderly, women and whoever was waiting for their turn had to wait for an extended period. Some told the king about their personal problems, but he turned a blind eye towards them. All he was worried about was the amount being collected from those villagers. I never expected such behaviour from him. I never saw or heard of an emperor such greedy and ignorant. Once again, I thought of killing him to bring back peace and order in the state but soon realised what I was thinking was not ethical and I regretted the influence of the evil on my mind.

MAHA-PUROHIT

Ministers and I secretly noticed Eklavya's emotions, and I could know that was the right day to tell him about our master plan. After that horrendous display of insensitivity and mercilessness was over, everybody including *Maharaj* retreated from the court. Ministers, few of those army men and I stayed back along with Eklavya.

"How do you feel?" questioned one of the ministers.

"I feel sad for them," he confessed.

"What should be the central dharma of human beings?" I asked.

"That man should serve in the name of God for the betterment of humankind. Those who lack knowledge must be educated, those who lack behaviour must be treated the way they are expected to treat others, those who do not show mercy must be welcomed with love and compassion," answered Eklavya.

"What about those who neither have wisdom, nor compassion and do not have any sentiments for fellow humans?" I asked.

"Those who neither progress nor let anyone progress must be separated from the community. Why would you ask that?" He was clueless.

"What if separation is not possible?" I further continued my questions.

"Those who can't be separated from the community shall be eliminated from the same to bring prosperity," he replied.

"Then remove the king!!" we all said at once.

"I must! What... No! What did you just say?" he was stunned to hear that.

"We have planned for a coup," one of the army men said.

"A coup... Why? What would you get from that?" he asked in shock.

"This king does not have any sense of judgement. He is brutal, careless and is lost in his majestic aspects. He neither progresses nor let anybody prosper. This king lacks knowledge, has lost his character and is devoid of any sensitivity towards his people. You just saw a glimpse his cruelty on innocent people that made you sad. Very sad! Moreover, he can't be separated from the community as he is the ruler. So, he must be eliminated! He should be overthrown from the crown to let Rudraputra regain its prosperity, to let its people live their lives peacefully!" that soldier replied, and Eklavya was trapped in his own argument and reasoning. He could not think of any other counter-argument and looked at me. I nodded my head up and down confirming and approving the idea of the coup against the king.

"Why me?! Why don't you kill him?" he then asked.

"He who kills the king will be a saviour for Rudraputra and its inhabitants. We are old now and have no desire to rule. Also, no one among us can come to an agreement of letting someone among us rule the state. We will, however, be with you at every point of your course of the rulership. People will have no objection, and the army would not retaliate either. They are used to obeying your orders now. Peace will return if you become the next king of the Rudraputra!" I explained to him, hoping that he would agree.

"I thought you were changed! I could not believe that you are still under the influence of the *Kali*. Moreover, your evil company made these people lose their minds as well. Killing him is not right, it is unethical. I can't do that, ever! And nobody is going to do that either!" he was worried.

"As a *Brahmin*, you just found yourself struggling with your arguments. Let's see if you can be a *Kshatriya*," I challenged him and further questioned,

"What are you expected to do as army chief of the nation?"

"That I must follow the royal orders and respect the rule. That I must, until my last breath, be determined to safeguard my nation, its people and resources from the enemies both internal and external," he replied with confidence.

"What if the former doesn't let you fulfil your latter dharma?" one of the ministers asked.

"If the administration causes harm to the integrity of the nation, maligns the peace of its people, a *Kshatriya* must adhere to his supreme dharma, that is safeguarding the interests of the country, its citizens and resources until the last breath. The latter must prevail!" he replied.

"Then fulfil your dharma as a *Kshatriya*! Protect the nation. Kill the king!" I encouraged him. Once again Eklavya was stunned to see every road going towards the same destination – the king's death.

"You are born with a purpose, Eklavya. Sometimes, you must lose a battle to win a war. Taking his life will save thousands of lives from being ended. His life is not worth living anyway. You were brought here by the destiny to fulfil this task. We were just deciding on the next king of Rudraputra.

Moreover, we were going to exercise the coup for sure, be it with you or without you! But remember, the aftermath of the rebellion will all be your responsibility then! It is desired that you take this responsibility and prevent a future uprising of the tension among the people. You are their hope, don't let their dream die. You very well know what it is to lose faith in life! Follow your dharma. It is the same king who is responsible for the death of those innocent villagers. It was his ignorant attitude that lead to Tara's death! It was the same king who never did anything for our farmers and Vyas had to go to another village to bring some seeds for agriculture. Neither Vyas would have gone there, nor Sumati would have died in vain. She was alone in that unsafe condition. Who knows she might have left this world in remorse and not because of the herbs I gave her. The king did not care about us! He never cared for you, your village and Ikshvakus, why should we care about him? Why should you care about him then?? You could have studied in your village if there was a *Gurukul* nearby. Then *Amma* would not have gone in distress in your memories, Vyas would not have been left alone, and he would be alive today! The universe is giving you this last chance of proving yourself, one last chance to do something for the people, one opportunity to kill the evil! Don't let it go! Don't let one more blame be on your head. Lord Krishna had to educate Arjuna about his dharma. In the same way, you are being shown the right path. There is nothing unethical in killing the king. He is the *Kali*, he is the evil! You, be the controller of the system and change it!" I was out of breath and sat in a chair in disappointment. I tried my best to deceive him somehow so that he could agree on taking the kingship of the state. My deception, this time was for a noble cause, and so I did not hesitate to mould my words.

"Hold your breath, *Maha-Mantri*. Is this the mind game you were talking about the other day at the cantonment?" Eklavya tried connecting the dots.

"No! Never!!" I shouted, and my voice echoed in the court. Suddenly, we all heard the opening of the doors and two guards came inside, leaving us all frozen as we thought our plan was leaked.

"You can't be worse than this king, nobody can be. Just do it! End this tyranny! Kill him! We all want this. Do it for us! Do it for the good of humanity," both the guards said that to Eklavya and everybody returned to their peace. He stood still, clueless and in trauma. Perhaps, he was almost prepared to get the task done.

"I know someone who can do this happily," he replied.

"They have been living in a constant terror of Rudraputra's attack on their tribe. They lost many of their members to the fight for their protection. Why not give this opportunity to them? It will ensure them their safety," he further suggested.

"Alright! What are you up to?" I asked.

"There is a tribe on the other side of the jungle. They have been a soft target for this king to expand his territory. Tribal people live in constant fear that one day the king will attack their settlement and occupy their land. I have been with them. Tara belonged to them!" Eklavya further explained, and few army men were in the captain's team the other evening and thus, knew about what he had just said, and they endorsed the plan.

"His next trip to the jungle for hunting will be his last!" Eklavya said, and we all conveyed our consensus with him.

It took a few days for us to prepare the plan of action. Eklavya made his trustworthy soldiers confident about the killing and consulted with me on the same. One morning, we all mounted on the horses equipped with all the weapons we could carry and proceeded to the jungle. Upon asking by some other guards about where they all were heading to, I told them it was for the safety and security tour. The kingdom often conducted such tours to ensure everything was alright in the region. It was also for sending a strong message to the enemy that messing up with the Royals would lead in their heavy destruction. The royal guards without any doubt trusted us, they didn't dare to stop their *Maha-Mantri* from doing so. Humungous gates of the palace were opened, and we went out in synchronisation. The king of Rudraputra slept fondly in his bedroom while we made plans to put him on sleep forever.

EKLAVYA

On my way for meeting the tribal king, I wondered how I ran for my life in the jungle a few weeks ago, starving, bleeding and screaming there. And now I was going with a great sense of pride and responsibility on my shoulders, sitting on a horse and with royal soldiers ensuring my safety from every possible danger. After crossing a few dried-up streams, miles of dense forest and admiring the wilderness, we entered the outer vicinity of the tribal village. Everything seemed to be normal outside. But, there were memories of the past throbbing inside my mind. I missed Tara badly, I remembered the day when she woke me up by sprinkling water on my face. I recalled how tribal soldiers imprisoned and dragged me to the *choupal*, I recalled my conversation with the tribal king before my execution, the sound of sharpening of the executioner's sword, people standing to see me being slaughtered, I remembered the fear that chilled my spine that day, I didn't forget any of that. Those memories gave me goosebumps.

Little after entering the outer vicinity, the troop reached into the village and saw the *choupal*. Tribal king was sitting on the throne, surrounded by his people. The executioner and bodyguards also stood nearby the throne. The king stopped addressing his people at the sight of me along with the royal soldiers mounted on horses. Though they all knew that something was wrong, nobody panicked as the movement of our regiment was subtle and seemed to have no intention of picking up a fight. The crowd gave way to the horses, I dismounted and climbed up the stage. I had serious conversations with the tribal king, explaining everything to him from right after escaping my execution to gaining the confidence of the Rudraputra kingdom.

At first, he could not believe that I was going to be the next king of the Rudraputra. But seeing royal army escorting me in the jungle made him believe what I just told. The tribe was happy to speculate on their freedom from the fear of being attacked. They became friends with us. However, they were sad after knowing that Tara had died. I did not tell them that it was she and her brother who released those animals and helped me escape from there. Though they wouldn't do any harm to me even after knowing the truth I didn't want them to curse Tara, and her brother. *Maha-Purohit*'s company was teaching me how to play with words. Perhaps, it was necessary for me to possess some diplomacy as I was the future king of Rudraputra.

A few days later the king desired to go to the jungle for hunting. As planned, I had already conveyed my plan to the tribal people. The king was accompanied by a few of his trusted men. Upon reaching the jungle, tribal people surrounded them. Those guards were few as compared to the tribe. The king of Rudraputra had no courage left to face his enemies. He looked here and there at his men for help. Soon, they all saw *Maha-Purohit*, ministers, some army men and me joining them. The king and his men were stunned.

"Eklavya! Kill them! They are our enemies!!" *Maharaj* commanded, but I did not move. The king of the tribe pulled *Maharaj* down from his horse.

"If you don't want to be killed with this man, go away! And don't ever dare to say anything to anybody about what is happening here," *Maha-Purohit* said to the so-called trusted men of the king. They all ran for their lives, leaving their master stranded in between of nowhere.

"We will take him away with us. He must not get an easy death!" said the tribal king.

"Tell your people that he was killed by a pride of lions in the jungle," he further suggested. Tribal people were cheering their win.

"Indeed, the pride of lion has captured the king!" I said to the tribal king, and they all laughed.

"Our best wishes for your crowning liturgy," they all wished me.

"Do visit us in the capital!" I said, and we left for the palace. The corrupt king of Rudraputra was taken away into the jungle in an unconscious state. Nobody knew his whereabouts after that.

28: The Crowning Liturgy

MAHA-PUROHIT

All those who left the palace came back except the *Maharaj*. Remarkably few people were aware of what had happened to him. The general population was busy working inside the palace, and nobody noticed his absence for a few hours. After preparing myself to share that news with the people, I summoned the palace staff and guards on duty inside the courtroom. Everyone gathered there in minutes. It was one of the rare occasions when an entire team of the palace was called to meet inside the courtroom. Generally, the king did that if someone had to get punished or if there was an emergency. After the arrival of all, I attained a position beside the throne. It was then when everybody noticed it vacant without their king sitting in it. Murmuring started in the groups.

"Silence! Please... I am about to share the sad news with you all. My heart is filled with tremendous remorse and grief. Dear fellow beings, we all have become orphans now. An accident that spanned its wings of wrath took away our beloved king from us in an instant! *Maharaj* is no more... He was killed by the pride of lions in the jungle!" I took a sobbing pause for a moment, wondering how I am going to carry on with the drama. There was a commotion in the courtroom. The majority of the people could not even believe that their king was dead suddenly. Royal courtesans and some other officials who were mere puppets in the hands of the king howled in deep grief.

"This royal escort will tell you what happened. He was there with *Maharaj* in the jungle," I pointed at one of the men whom I had warned in the jungle about not to share what had happened there. That man shivered with trauma, somehow climbing up the stage to do the melodramatic talking.

"This morning, *Maharaj* told us about his plan for going into the jungle for hunting. As usual, few of our men accompanied him during the hunting amusement. We used to go with the king for his protection. He always hunted within the safe range of the jungle. With almost no chance of any severe threat to his life in that part of the forest, we went few in number and carried limited weapons with us today. Little did we know that our false sense of safety would turn into the biggest nightmare in the history of Rudraputra! *Maharaj* never saw any lion in the outskirts of the jungle before. All wild animals live reasonably inside the wilderness. But today, he spotted a lion there and could not resist his desire to hunt that. In excitement, he kicked his horse and chased that lion further into the jungle. We followed him along. I reminded him of the danger of getting attacked by any wild animal inside the jungle, but he ignored my warning and kept on following the lion. The lion was alone and afraid to see many of us and ran for his life.

Maharaj got even excited to see that lion running away from him. After few minutes, what we all saw left us dreaded! That lion took us near his pride. It was then when *Maharaj* realised the dangerousness of the situation. In desperation, he ordered us to turn around and run. We reminded him that doing so would provoke the pride to chase us and hunt us down, but he did not listen and rode his horse away from the lions. Lions noticed him and assumed him as their prey running away from them in distress. The pride chased him too. Seeing the situation going out of control, we only had that opportunity to save our lives, and we retreated in the opposite direction. Lions attacked his horse by that time. We could not do anything, we were constrained! We heard a loud, painful scream seconds after we began running away. Nothing else was ever heard from *Maharaj* after that. We mourn the tragic demise of our great king! Rudraputra has not only lost its king, but its guardian today. We all have become orphans!" concluded the man and he went down the stage.

Ministers, those army men and I were amazed to hear the speech. I was impressed by the cooperation shown by him to us. But we all pretended as if we were genuinely shattered after the demise of our 'courageous' ruler.

"Please don't lose your calm and handle yourself in this tragic time! We all must take care of each other. *Maharaj* would have wanted us to handle this situation boldly and with courage. He would expect us to show maturity. Please do not panic. May Lord be with Rudraputra and may *Maharaj's* soul rest in peace!" I showed my sympathies to the people.

"Our kingdom must choose its new king. In the absence of any heir to the throne, it is vital to elect one member from the royal palace with the consensus of *Maha-Mantri*, the cabinet and approved army men. We all have made our agreement with Eklavya being the new king of Rudraputra. He is presently serving as an army in charge of the state. We all have seen his capabilities, morals and principles and we think he would be able to take our motherland to new heights," I proposed Eklavya's name for the crown. There arose a disturbance inside the courtroom.

Civilians gathered outside the palace by then. The news of king's demise spanned a jungle fire. People wanted to know the reason for their *Maharaj's* death and that who was going to be their next king. Messengers from the court were said to inform them about Eklavya's liturgy and the sudden demise of the king in the jungle. I along with other priests of the state participated in the ceremony.

EKLAVYA

Things happened so fast that I could not understand what was going on with me. A few days ago, I was there in the jungle hoping that the tribal people would spare my life. I ran here and there in search of shelter and food. Few days before, I struggled to prove myself eligible for the post of the army in charge, and now I would become the king. It all seemed like a weird dream to me. Rather, my entire life was like a bizarre tide that took over my mind and sometimes, let my mind took over itself. A nightmare that haunted and at the same time encouraged me, incited love in me, induced hatred and pacified me, made me angry, gave me hope, broke my heart and what not! After some traditional ceremonies, *Maha-Purohit* asked me to come after him. We were followed by the rest of the staff. He, upon reaching near a big balcony of the palace faced the public standing below on the ground shouting and growling in doubt, anger, fear and anxiety. He folded his hands and began saying,

"Greetings! Dear inhabitants of Rudraputra, the course of time is such that I can't even express my joy to see you all here. The palace is grieving for its irreplaceable loss. But we must understand that God's will is firm. If this is what he wants, then be it! Rudraputra flourished under the supervision of *Maharaj*. His sudden death has left us clueless in the middle of nowhere! It is time we take courage and co-operate with the state. In this difficult hour, we must not lose our hope for a bright future. Nobody has ever cheated death, nobody will ever cheat death for death is not the last sleep. Instead, it is the final awakening of the soul. King's body might have left us, but his spirit will remain immortal forever. His love will be with us for eternity. Rudraputra can't thank him enough for his incredible headship of the state. Now that we had to abide by the laws he created, Rudraputra has a new leader! We have a new emperor! Bow to the king! Oo... Rudraputra! Bow to emperor Eklavya, the son of Vyas and the Scion of Ikshvaku!!" *Maha-Purohit* announced and commanded.

"Long live the king! Long live Rudraputra!... Hail Eklavya!... Hail Rudraputra!" people began enchanting slogans. With hope in their hearts that Rudraputra would see its golden days, they all celebrated the moment with pomp and show. I now got the sense of my power and responsibility that came with it. I came closer to the balcony and folded my hands in gratitude. People never saw their previous king acknowledging their support for the kingdom before. My simple act of appreciation left everyone optimistic about the end of *Kali Yuga* and the beginning of a golden age in Rudraputra.

"By accepting God as a witness, deeming the five elements of water, air, fire, sky and soil as a witness and by taking all the people here as witnesses... I, Eklavya and the emperor of Rudraputra, at this moment, take the oath of devoting my life to the prosperity of the state. In the light of the constitution and human morals, I will act for maintaining the peace and order in the state. As a *Brahmin*, I am bound to propagate wisdom in my state...I am ready to rejuvenate the education system of Rudraputra... It is my religion as the King to be among the vanguard of the defence of the country. Hence, I as a *Kshatriya* assure you that I will protect my land and its people from enemies, both internal and external!... It is unquestionable that to strive for the overall betterment of the state, monetary flow is required. Therefore, I take a vow of being with the *Vaishyas* always! I must work for the upliftment of the business class of Rudraputra. I will serve the interest of the service class of the state. If *Shudras* of Rudraputra need my help of any kind or in any way, I will put my constant effort in assisting them. At last, I would like to tender my humble request to the stalwarts of my state to co-operate with me in this journey of hope and light. Together, we can make Rudraputra great again. With that being said, I wish I could be an efficient reigning monarch of Rudraputra! I seek your blessings and best wishes for that!" I finished talking and waved in contentment.

The enthusiasm people showed for me was enormous. Seemed as if nobody cared if the previous king was dead. Everyone congratulated each other. That evening essentially marked the downfall of the *Kali* (evil) in Rudraputra and ensured the virtues of the golden age. Soon, People retreated towards their homes. Staff members prepared for the celebration in the palace. Everyone including *Maha-Purohit* cheered except for me as I was lost in another world, thinking how Father, Maa, *Amma*, the old man and Tara would have felt if they were alive to see me reaching impeccable heights. I wiped the tears from my eyes and proceeded towards the court to join my people in the celebration.

Figure: Maha-Purohit crowning Eklavya, the new king of Rudraputra.

29: All's Well That Ends Well

MAHA-PUROHIT

Rudraputra flourished gradually after Eklavya's royal rectification. As promised, he worked for all the classes in the society and believed in equality and sovereignty. Though he did not believe in any religion yet, he treated people following different faiths with the same respectful attitude. He would always sit and discuss the critical decisions for the state with me and the cabinet. His office included experts from every field. Rudraputra had women ministers too! Since Eklavya did not have any desire to exploit stately resources for gaining personal privileges, all the money was utilised for the advancement of the nation. The cabinet then realised how much progress could be attained if the previous king had a controlled desire for carnal delights.

Eklavya and all other people who knew what had happened with the king in the jungle had no remorse left in their hearts for his death. Those who were still unaware of the coup had forgotten if there ever was some other king in the state. The glory of the kingdom reached neighbouring countries as well. And so, Rudraputra developed a bond of friendship with other kingdoms over the years. That even empowered the people and their resources. The tribal king and his tribe became great allies of Rudraputra. They no longer had to live in fear of getting their settlement destroyed and captured.

EKLAVYA

Few months went by quickly. One day, I desired to visit the village where I was born. I summoned the army chief and asked him to arrange for the tour. Upon reaching there, I found that most of the elderly people died already. Things changed a lot in those nine years of my absence. I had turned into an adult, and my appearance differed a lot than what I used to be when I was thirteen. Youngsters could not recognise me and those who did were afraid and embarrassed by their deeds of throwing me out of the village. But I had no grudges for them. Instead, I asked if Ikshvakus needed anything. Seeing me turned into a king was enough for them to feel proud. One of their clan members was now the head of the state. What else could they ask for? I spoke with a few remaining elders, visited my abandoned house, assuring my people that I would be available for them in case anybody needed anything to be done.

While retreating for the kingdom, I also visited the cemetery and discovered that those people whom I had given the charge for the cemetery managed it well. I stood for some time near the grave of the old man and his wife. It was then when I recalled my conversation with Mohammad, feeling a chill in my spine. After giving some money to those managers for renovating the cemetery, I with my regiment left for the palace. On my way back to the castle, I kept on thinking about Mohammad and was wondering why I haven't heard from him after he left me in the cemetery.

MAHA-PUROHIT

With each passing day, Eklavya's glory and Rudraputra's prosperity grew and ascended by leaps and bounds. Many marriage proposals from reputed kingdoms arrived for him. How could neighbouring kings let a man this great and powerful go? They all wanted him for their daughters. Moreover, their daughters were also very much interested in getting married to the warrior king. But Eklavya had to fulfil his father's dream of creating the world devoid of any artificial misery. And so, he did not want to let his personal responsibilities hinder his course of action as the king of Rudraputra. Besides, his inner quest of realising true-self and God remained partially unfulfilled. He, no matter how eligible he was, kept on refusing those proposals. Not that he took a vow of practising *Bhramcharya* or something. Eklavya was just not ready yet.

Due to the unique influence of Eklavya on his people, neighbouring states also adopted his way to rule their kingdom. Rulers became reasonable and sensible; they took off the taxes. Kings saw it as their duty to promote spirituality and equality. The behaviour of animosity among the armies of different states vanished. Sins ceased to exist while virtues increased exponentially. Elders were respected, their teachings were appreciated, and followers of truth wrested the control from all the sinners, and put it in the path of ultimate redemption. The evil finally ceased to exist in the state. The universe gave

Eklavya all that happiness which he was denied off until then. *Kali Yuga*, for a while, ended entirely in Rudraputra.

One beautiful day, Eklavya and I were wandering in the lush greenery of the royal garden, discussing upon reframing and amending the policies for better understanding and implementation. I saw someone coming towards me and we stopped our discussion and walking. Soon it was known that *Sarpanch* of one of the villages was approaching.

"Greetings! to the king and *Maha-Mantri*," he said while folding his hands.

"Welcome to the capital *Sarpanch Ji*. What brought you here? Is everything alright?" asked Eklavya while being concerned.

"Everything is perfectly fine by the grace of almighty. I just came here to meet you and express my gratitude for whatever you have done for my village," he said.

"Vyas went to his village for collecting some seeds for agriculture and had stayed at his house on the night of your birth," I told Eklavya.

"What?" His eyes opened wide in sudden reaction. He looked into the eyes of the *Sarpanch*.

"I did not know he is the son of Vyas! I had heard about him even before he came into this world!" *Sarpanch* and Eklavya hugged each other.

"Vyas suddenly remembered the prediction of *Maha-Purohit* and was eager to go back to his village. The night was violent, and no sailor was there to take him to the other side. He had to spend the night with me. He told me about the predictions *Maha-Purohit* made about your birth. And as I can see, his predictions took shape and became real!" *Sarpanch* was mesmerised, I smiled gently.

"Tell me what he said about me?" Eklavya insisted.

"The entire region will witness a wave of contentment after the birth of that child... Vyas will be blessed with prosperity. The child would be known for his compassion and will to serve humanity," *Sarpanch* recalled Vyas's statement of me telling the nature of Eklavya's birth.

"However, there will come, a time when the child's views and actions will go opposite to what is deemed 'fit' in this society. There will be a time when he will try to destroy social stigma and traditional practices for the greater good of the world... It would be then when he is out-casted from this society and by its people, it is my understanding," he further added. Eklavya constantly looked at both of us. I believe, he was amazed to listen to that prediction which proved itself to be true so far.

"The child will possess incredible willpower and knowledge to learn every type of skill and competence... The scion of Ikshvaku will be born to fulfil God's will of protecting the righteous. He will rise to power and influence. His birth may not seem to be special, but his death will create history. He would have the ability to learn archery and other combat skills just by watching. Hence the name of the child shall be Eklavya! Eklavya, he who learns bow by watching. Prepare for his arrival, we all shall celebrate and welcome him with great pomp and show! That was all I could recall from the past," *Sarpanch* said with a smile.

"All that was said by *Maha-Purohit* turned out to be true. No matter how events unfolded into your life Son, the result is certainly as per him... You were celebrated for your birth in the entire village. You had excellent skills and incredible learning potential. You were out-casted from your community. There were times when you tried to end your life, but destiny did not let you end it as you were born to do something great! From the beginning, you are fighting for the righteous. And now that you have gained influence and power this world must keep prospering," *Sarpanch* linked every prediction to real events that happened in Eklavya's life. Everything made sense. Eklavya was left awestruck.

"So, that was it! That was how destiny had planned my life to be?" He was puzzled.

"For all these years, I struggled to discover the purpose of my life. I was in constant search for the reason why I could not end my life despite trying for so many times. Those mysterious people... Mohammad and Mahavir, they were not just people! Every good and bad event unfolded its purpose before me that I could not see!" Eklavya further realised.

"I am glad that you came, *Sarpanch Ji*! Please don't leave without having some food," he folded his hands, bidding farewell before he left for the courtroom. *Sarpanch* proceeded towards the royal kitchen, and I stood there for a moment, thinking about what Eklavya would do next knowing that my prediction about him had turned true for the most part.

He kept my father in his house the night before my birth, and there I stood right outside that house in front of the same person."

-   Eklavya (*Long Live the Sullied*)

Epilogue

TIME

Such is this saga of light in the dark epoch. The adventure of hope in sheer atrocity and a story of life emerging out of nothing. It is the birth of a dream after reality runs out. It is the rise of Eklavya, the warrior king, the son of Vyas and the scion of Ikshvaku.

"Nothing comes easy in this world, and everything has a price. What comes swiftly will go quickly; only that which grows slowly endures. Appreciate the hard times you get in the life, for great things emerge from the darkness sometimes. It has been rightly said that you will get run over even if you are sitting on the right track. Just sitting is the death of progression and progression is life. Don't let the fear of being lost keep you from exploring your world, both inner and outer. Lost are those who never dared to get out from their homes. Inject your existence with activity. Counsel not your feelings of trepidation but rather your expectations and your fantasies. Try not to sit and wait for miracles to happen. Get it going, make your own future. Shape your own expectation. Create your own adoration. What's more, whatever your convictions may be, embrace your creator, respect his creations! You shall make the most of this life, Son. May Almighty bless you, may Rudraputra live long!" said Eklavya in a shaky subtle voice before leaving the kingdom and enlightened the new acting-king of Rudraputra. After putting the crown on the head of the new king, he bowed to him, to the ministers and to the people attending the ceremony.

After serving for eight glorious years to Rudraputra as a king, thirty-years-old Eklavya was all set to begin his journey once again to realise *Brahman* and true-self. Rudraputra had gained much glory under his rule of eight years than it had nurtured ever before. Eklavya saw many of his loved ones departing from the world, he fought many wars to protect the nation and nurtured his people as if a titan was cultivating the realms of the universe. He firmly stood by his oath he had taken in the swearing ceremony about eight years ago. During his last days of kingship, he handed over the powers and responsibilities of the state to one of the most eligible men democratically chosen by the royal members. The new king was none other than Bheema's son, Bibhatsu.

The council was opposed to his decision of leaving the kingdom, initially. It was only when he promised he will come back in need of the hour that he was given the consensus of the cabinet and *Maha-Purohit* to go on a spiritual voyage. Bibhatsu was chosen to serve the kingdom until Eklavya returns after gaining higher consciousness through his spiritual pursuit. As Eklavya retreated, entire capital bewailed, for their great king was going for who knows how many years. What happened to him after his departure remained unknown to Rudraputra.

Bibhatsu, under the supervision of *Maha-Purohit*, ruled the kingdom, trying his best to follow Eklavya's teachings. However, a year later after Eklavya departed from the kingship of Rudraputra, good was on the decline. *Kali* was extending its arms in the state. People got entangled in mutual friction with each passing day. Rudraputra became the same barren land with its inhabitants devoid of any civic sense. The cycle of time turned upside down, and the world witnessed the chaos. Those who remained honest and genial were disassociated from the community and savagery started rising. Spiritual desires of the people degenerated, and individuals who knew nothing about religion dared to talk about moral standards. Dharma shattered, and hands of malice effortlessly did awful in the world. The evil spanned its wings wide in *Gurukul*s as well.

"I cannot pay so much. I am a small farmer and need money for agriculture too. Please reduce the amount you are asking me to pay for their education! I beg you!" Poor farmer joining hands before the head of the *Gurukul* requested for his child to be admitted.

"That which applies to all will apply to you too. We can't do anything, either pay or go back right now! Don't come here ever again without money!" One of the *Acharya*s shouted.

"You cannot ask for this unfair amount!" the farmer was frustrated. "Gone are the days when *Gurukul*s followed (Adi) Shankaracharya's principles. It is us who define its existence now. How dare you speak to me like that? Who do you think you are? God?" *Acharya* was under the influence of the evil.

"I am Gandharv! The son of Kashyap and scion of Ikshvaku." The man replied with pride, the same pride Eklavya used to bear with his legacy. The so-called gurus laughed at his answer and kicked him out of the *Gurukul*.

Sobbing children were terrified by the behaviour of those corrupt *Acharyas*, and they followed along with the farmer silently. Finding himself not being able to feed his family properly and educate his children in the *Gurukul*, the farmer loathed himself in disgust.

"You both head to home, I have some work to do in the fields," he ordered his sons, and they retreated. With lost hope and no desire to live that kind of life, poor farmer proceeded towards the Ganges to end his life.

The farmer stood on the river-bank and felt a shiver in his weak body. Ganga flowed with tremendous rage that afternoon, warning the farmer of its dangerous swirling depths. The brutal might of Ganga's icy water seemed to be the perfect coffin for him. He folded his hands, and with his eyes closed recited last prayers. He folded his legs to gain some thrust for the jump and embraced for his death.

"*Om shanti, shanti, shanti, om,*" he chanted and...

"Excuse me, I am lost! Could you please help me find my way?" someone shouted, and farmer opened his eyes, losing the impulse toward jumping into the river. He looked back and asked,

"Who are you?"

"My name is Mohammad," replied the other person. And by the perfect forces of the destiny, one more undeserved death was postponed that day for the rise of the chosen one!

~

An Episode from Long Live the Sullied

The royal guards stood at the hinged heavy metallic door, holding spears in their hands to prevent anyone without authorisation from entering the royal palace that day. The palace had always been open to the public for meeting with the cabinet and Eklavya, their king. But something tragic happened last night that doomed the kingdom, immediately resulting in restricted access policy in effect. No outsider was allowed unless accompanying any minister or the king himself. And it was the reason why the guards resisted *Acharya* Virbhadra from entering the palace to go meet the king. {portion skimmed through}

While on his way to the royal court, *Acharya* Virbhadra asked the *Maha-Mantri* about what was it that tormented the palace in a sudden span of one night, why Eklavya was called immediately to the palace and why everyone including *Maha-Mantri* looked so tensed. *Maha-Mantri* looked at *Acharya* and asked him to see for himself what happened last night, advising him that he just arrived at the palace in wrong time. He further said that whatever was inside had already made many workers and ministers lose their wits at the very sight of it, cautioning Acharya to be prepared to endure the gore he was about to witness. Despite being a fierce warrior and a yogi, *Acharya* felt a chill in his spine as he entered the hallway to the royal court.

What was it that doomed the state of Rudraputra? Why was Eklavya called immediately to the palace? What gore *Maha-Mantri* talked about with *Acharya* Virbhadra? And what made people who witnessed it lose their senses? Only time would reveal…